WITHDRAWN

A Paris Affair

Also by Tatiana de Rosnay

Sarah's Key
A Secret Kept
The House I Loved
The Other Story

A Paris Affair

Tatiana de Rosnay

TRANSLATED FROM THE FRENCH BY SAM TAYLOR

St. Martin's Press ❧ New York

A PARIS AFFAIR. Copyright © 2014 by Éditions Héloise d'Ormesson. Translation copyright © 2015 by Sam Taylor. All rights reserved. Printed in the United States of America. For information, address St. Martin's Press, 175 Fifth Avenue, New York, N.Y. 10010.

www.stmartins.com

The Library of Congress Cataloging-in-Publication Data is available upon request.

ISBN 978-1-250-06880-4 (hardcover)
ISBN 978-1-4668-7739-9 (e-book)

St. Martin's Press books may be purchased for educational, business, or promotional use. For information on bulk purchases, please contact the Macmillan Corporate and Premium Sales Department at 1-800-221-7945, extension 5442, or write to specialmarkets@macmillan.com.

First published in France under the title *Son Carnet Rouge* by Éditions Héloise d'Ormesson in 2014.

First U.S. Edition: July 2015

10 9 8 7 6 5 4 3 2 1

For Catherine, Chantal, Frédérique,

Julia, Laure, and Valérie

Contents

❦

So, my sweet, what are you complaining about?
Your husband isn't faithful?
But men are never faithful.

—ANDRÉ MAUROIS (1885–1967), *Climates*

A Paris Affair

Hotel Room

After an Edward Hopper (1882–1967)
painting of the same name
For C.B.R.

There are good marriages,
but there are no delicious ones
—François de La Rochefoucauld
(1613–1680), *Maxims*

My beauty,

I imagine you reading this letter, which I slipped under the door while you were already in the room, waiting for me. I could have just sent you an e-mail or a text, but I prefer writing these pages to you by hand. As you unfold them, you will not understand at first. We know by heart the shapes of our bodies and the textures of our skin, but you have never seen my handwriting, nor I yours.

This room. This room where we have met so

many times over the past four years. The wood-paneled walls, the high window, the green velvet wing chair, the mahogany chest of drawers. By now, you must have undressed: your clothes are folded on the chair, your high heels abandoned on the floor. Your cloche hat, which you wear so you can walk past Reception "incognito" and which suits you so well, has been casually tossed on the console table. You are wearing something a little risqué, perhaps that pink babydoll, which shows off your shoulders and your waist. Your legs are bare, and I can see your shapely thighs, your slender ankles, as if I were there.

But I am not there. I have not come to meet you because our affair is over. I can sense the muscles tensing around your eyes as you read that last line, and I feel bad. I am a coward, because I prefer not to have to face your reaction in person.

For a long time, I thought I could control our affair. You were a breath of fresh air, a delicious parenthesis. But you have taken up too much space in my existence. You now represent a danger. I am swamped by you. I am married, I have three children. You, too, have your husband and your little ones. For the last four years, our secret garden allowed me to get away. But the feeling is too strong.

You could be the love of my life. The woman all men dream of, the woman a man will give everything for. When I wake up in the morning, I think of you. When I go to sleep at night, my last thought is of you. All day long, I imagine you at work, with your colleagues. I have come to realize that I am obsessed by you.

You must be wondering why I am writing this nonsense, instead of being there with you, making love to you. You are probably angry, pacing the room with your long dancer's legs, muttering to yourself, "What a jerk!" You're right.

I could pursue our relationship, continuing to meet you, and to lie. But I am leaving you, and no one will ever know anything about it, because our affair is a secret. Our joys and our sufferings belong to the shadows, our pleasures, too. We were clandestine lovers. Only this hotel room knows the truth. If the walls had voices, they would tell our story.

❧

He slipped the letter under the door and hurtled down the staircase, heart in his mouth. He scurried down into the Métro, and took a train back to his office. He was sweating. He was suffocating. All his thoughts circled back to Gabrielle in that room, reading his letter. Yes, it had been cowardly, his sneaking around and his running, but facing up to her would have taken more strength than he possessed. How could he resist Gabrielle? No man could. He had done what he had to. He'd cut it short. He'd broken up with her. There was no other choice. He felt relieved now, knowing he would no longer need to lie to his wife. A terrible weight had been lifted from his shoulders. Good-bye, Gabrielle. She would tear up the letter in a fury, then get dressed and leave the hotel discreetly. He had nothing to fear. No one knew anything. No one would ever know. He would continue to be the irreproachable François: the loving and faithful husband, the kind and gentle father.

All the same, he thought about her possible reactions. Would she stoop to phoning him, to find out his reasons? No, he felt sure, there would be no questions. He had explained it all in his letter. It was a well-written letter, he thought. Elegant. Honest. Perhaps she would keep it? He hadn't signed it, nor had he used her name. He had been cunning: he'd written it by hand, but not in his usual calligraphy. A few years from now, Gabrielle would reread it, a tender smile at the corners of her lips. Ah, François . . . She would remember. The caresses, the embraces, the acts of love in that room, on that bed. He would remember, too.

❧

François arrived at his office. He greeted a few colleagues. Loosening his tie, he gulped down some water, then sat in front of his computer. Glanced at the clock. Two thirty. She had undoubtedly left the hotel by now. Gone to eat lunch. She must have called a friend and admitted with a laugh, "Some idiot stood me up," without revealing his identity, because, after all, she was married, too, and had to be discreet. Usually after making love, they would drink a glass of champagne together, and nibble a few petits fours. Exquisite moments. How beautiful she was, lying languid on the bed, her lips pink and moist, her breasts bare. He was going to miss Gabrielle's breasts. He remembered that he hadn't eaten anything, and asked his assistant to order him some sushi.

He ate at his desk, eyes riveted to his computer screen. He worked mechanically. After an hour, he checked his cell phone. No messages. He couldn't help feeling disappointed, even a little worried. She hadn't even tried to get ahold of him. Had she at least read his letter? Was she still waiting for him, sitting on the bed in her babydoll? Had he slipped the letter under the carpet by mistake? Or maybe he'd gotten the wrong room? He hadn't thought about that possibility. Perhaps he should send her a text? No, that would be ridiculous.

He stood up and looked out the window, only one thought in his head: Gabrielle in the hotel room, growing impatient, Gabrielle, who had not read the letter. But what was he thinking? Of course she had read it. She hadn't been in touch because she was furious, hurt. It was true: he had been a coward. But it was too late now. What's done is done, he thought. He ought to concentrate on his work. Forget the hotel room.

Standing at the coffee machine, a female colleague asked him if he'd heard the news.

"What news?" he said.

"The building that burned to the ground."

"No! Where?"

"In Paris! This afternoon! Have you been living under a rock or something?"

She pointed to the conference room, where the entire office—about twenty people—was crowded around a television screen. A rolling news channel was showing images of a building consumed by flames, half-concealed by thick black smoke. He moved closer, holding his cup of coffee. Words scrolled past on the ticker at the bottom of the screen: FIRE IN A PARIS HOTEL—TWO DEAD, SEVERAL MISSING—TEN INJURED, FOUR IN CRITICAL CONDITION. Suddenly he recognized the street, and the hotel, and he dropped his cup. The black liquid pooled over the linoleum floor.

He couldn't speak. All the color had drained from his face. He stood frozen in front of the screen, in a daze. The newscaster's voice was explaining that the cause of the fire was unknown. It had started just after 1:00 pm and had spread with unimaginable speed. Part of the roof had collapsed. And yet the hotel had been recently renovated, so there was no suggestion that it had been unsafe. Could it have been an electrical fault? Or a deliberate act? There would be an investigation. For now, two people were dead, but that figure might still rise. The fire was not yet under control. Hundreds of firefighters and police were at the scene. The entire quarter had been sealed off.

He staggered back to his desk. His mouth was dry and he could hardly breathe. He picked up his cell phone. She was listed in his address book under a man's name: GABRIEL. The phone rang a few times: then her voice said, "Hello, please leave a message," in that slightly abrupt way of hers that he loved so much. My God, how could he hear her voice when she was perhaps seriously burned, trapped under rubble, dying or dead?

He paced the office in a fever. How could such a thing have happened? The fire must have started just after he left. She had been waiting for him. For him. The room was on the fifth floor. Had she had time to escape? Was she standing outside on the street in her babydoll? Or worse, was she in the morgue? He thought, with horror, of her husband. He didn't know the man at all. Didn't even know what he looked like. And her children. Still young, like his. How would the children get through this ordeal?

He realized he couldn't stay in the office. Making an excuse about a last-minute meeting, he left. Once again, he took the Métro, this time back to the scene of the tragedy. During the trip, he thought of her, of the terror she must have felt when the smoke began seeping under the door. The panic. The dread. The flames. What was he going to do? He didn't even know her address. All he knew was that she lived in the Latin Quarter, near Rue Monge. Beyond that, he knew very little about her. She was a secretive woman. The hotel room had been their world. Their universe.

As soon as he reached the neighboring street, the awful smell of the fire filled his nostrils. The smoke was still rising, black plumes in the sky. Police roadblocks had been set up in various places, obstructing his passage. There were crowds of onlookers. All he could do was stand there, crushed, staring at the smoke. He tried to call her again. Three rings, then voice mail. Should he send her a text anyway? Ask how she was? He didn't dare. It was impossible to know who had her cell phone at this moment. If he sent a message, a firefighter or a policeman might read it.

A secret affair. No one knew anything. Ever. Not her husband, not his wife.

He went home in a wretched state. His wife, concerned, asked if he was all right. He replied tonelessly that he had a headache. She gave him a pill. Before dinner, he watched the news. The two fatalities were both women. He thought he was going to faint. He had to confess everything now. Reveal the truth before the police or her husband found out. He had paid for the room with a credit card in his name, François R. And what about the hotel's security cameras? Even if they had been destroyed, the videos were stored somewhere else. He would almost certainly be seen entering the hotel, just before the fire broke out. The investigators would track him down. He would have to explain himself. Tell them the story of his and Gabrielle's four-year affair, the pink babydolls, the champagne, the petits fours. Disclose their meetings in the hotel room. (How many had there been? He'd lost count.) He would have to make public their most private moments, exposing memories of Gabrielle's shapely thighs, her breasts, her body, her husky voice when she spoke during sex, and the arousing recollection of her pleasure, the smell of her hair, the taste of her lips, memories that belonged only to him. No more lying. He would confess everything. Pluck up the courage to go and talk to his wife, here and now, while she was preparing dinner, and explain it all to her. No delays. No more waiting for the inevitable. He stood up, white as a sheet, his limbs shaky. She was in the kitchen, making a pot-au-feu. His wife. Anne. A nice girl. Still beautiful. Distinguished. Three children. A perfect family that would be blown to pieces. He imagined the gossip, the mudslinging. The sideways looks. His in-laws. His parents.

"I need to speak to you."

"You look so sad!"

"There's something I have to tell you."

He closed the kitchen door. There was no point getting the kids mixed up in this.

With trembling hands, he poured himself a glass of wine. He couldn't rid his mind of the vision of the babydoll and the morgue. He saw Anne's expression become troubled as she waited for him to speak. He drank the wine down in a single swallow.

"What's the matter with you?"

Staring at the refrigerator—that old, humming fridge—he began his confession in a monotone voice that she must surely find pitiable. Eyes glued in turn to the packet of cereal and then the toaster, he poured out his pathetic tale, his breath coming in short bursts. Gazing at the Post Office calendar pinned to the wall, he described the meeting in a restaurant, one spring day, the rendezvous, the lies, the hotel, the fire, the morgue. He spared her no details. There would, he knew, be a before and an after. He would remember this moment for the rest of his life.

His wife was pale. Her mouth hung open, and her fingers held tightly to a chair. She did not say a word. She scrutinized him with huge black eyes. Never had her eyes been so big or so dark.

An absolute silence filled the kitchen. Even the fridge had stopped humming. Time seemed suspended.

Anne got up suddenly, opened the door, and ran to the bathroom at the other end of the hallway.

He heard her throwing up. He remained standing in the middle of the room, distraught. Would this moment never end? It was unbearable.

His cell phone vibrated in his pocket. Nervously, he picked it up.

The screen flashed up a text from GABRIEL.

> Completely forgot our meeting! I'm in NYC, jetlagged. Hope you're not too mad at me! Are you free next Friday?

THE TEXTS

It's no easy feat getting intoxicated
with a glass of water and resisting
a bottle of rum.
  —GUSTAVE FLAUBERT (1821–1880), *Notebooks*

Hello, is this SOS Couples in Distress? . . . Yes, madame. I'm calling because I—Exactly. . . . It's very simple. Something incredible happened to me—Yes, something incredibly horrible, and I have to talk about it. I have to tell someone, and there is no way I can tell my mother, so when I saw your ad on the Internet, I thought: why not you? So . . . shall I tell you about my problem? . . . Okay . . . It's hard to know where to begin, or how to explain this. . . . Yes, I'll try to calm down. . . . Take a deep breath? Okay, let me try. . . . All right. So . . . I'm married. I'm thirty years old. My name is Emma. Oh, you don't want to know my name? Okay. Anyway, I have a child, who is almost two.

So, that's my life. You can't see me, so I'll describe myself:
I'm a brunette with dark eyes, pink cheeks—Oh, you're
not interested in my appearance either? I'm sorry. What
are you supposed to do when you learn that your husband
is cheating on you? I apologize for asking you that so
abruptly, but that's why I called. What should I do now?
It may seem like a dumb question, and I hope you're not
laughing at me—I know it's stupid, it's banal; I know. Husbands are always cheating on their wives. That's what everyone says. We're given enough warnings, aren't we, when
we're little girls? We see our father cheating on our mother,
our uncle cheating on our aunt, our grandfather cheating
on our grandmother. . . . Yes, we know all that, of course, but
when it's your own husband, the man you said yes to, blushing deeply in a church full of flowers, wearing a beautiful
white dress, the man who gave you a child and who plans to
have more children with you, the same man who says he
loves you and who is so kind, so tender, who even takes
out the trash and knows how to change a diaper—Please
don't laugh! I heard you giggling then. No, this isn't funny.
And I just wasn't expecting it. I didn't want to expect it. I
wanted to believe that my marriage would not be like all
the others. Other women's husbands might cheat and cheat
again, but not mine. Not my husband. And yet, that's exactly what he did—my own husband. He cheated on me. I'm
one of those wives who everyone pities—How did I find
out? Oh, so you do want to know that? Well, I'll tell you. I'll
tell you if you stop smiling. . . . Yes, I'm absolutely sure that
you are—I can hear it in your voice—and I don't think this is

funny at all. Anyway . . . yes . . . I found some texts on his
cell phone—Was I spying on him? Not at all! I'm not like
that. Absolutely not. But his cell phone was just lying
around. . . . Well, let's just say I wanted to tidy up. He's
pretty disorganized, my husband. I wanted to pick up his
office, and I noticed that he'd forgotten his cell phone there.
I took a look at it, that's all. Texts from a woman . . . love
messages. . . . You suspected as much? Really, is it that
common? Texts that haven't been deleted? . . . Oh, okay.
Why did he leave his cell phone in such an obvious place? I
have no idea. If I had a lover, and there were compromising
texts on my phone, I would never leave it lying around—
What's that? You think he wanted me to see them? He
wants me to know that he's cheating on me? I don't follow
you. Why would he want me to know? . . . Sorry? What are
you saying? Because he . . . because he doesn't love me anymore? No, I'm not saying anything else because I don't
know what to say. I'm just blown away by what you're telling
me—Did I take notes about the texts? Yes, of course. I cop-
ied them all down. . . . Read them to you? All right. Hang
on a minute. Okay. . . . 'My love, oh, my lover, the memory
of those moments still burns within me. I live only for our
next passionate meeting.' And it goes on: 'You are the king of
my nights. You are my prince, my god, my sovereign, and I
am your love slave.' No, there's more, I'm afraid: 'Yes, you
are the most beautiful lover in the world. You fill me with
such delight. Every time I say your name, I feel a thrill run
through my entire body.' His name is Gustave. Oh, you find
that thrilling, too? 'I'll wait for you at the usual place. I am

madly in love with you. I can't be without you. You drive me crazy. I will kiss you passionately, all over your body. Your loving and adoring Lili.' Yes, they're all signed 'Lili. Your adoring Lili'! Ridiculous, isn't it? Who is this Lili? I don't know anyone named Lili. And I haven't found anyone named Elisa or Liliane or Eulalie or Magali or even Valérie in the address book on his computer. So, who can she be, this Lili? A girl he met at work? Someone I know, hiding behind a false name? As for the usual place, I imagine it's her apartment. It can't be *my* home, anyway, because I'm here all the time—A hotel? You think so? A love hotel? Yes, I know what you mean but, really, I can't imagine Gustave in a love hotel. He's not a love hotel kind of guy—What *is* a love hotel kind of guy? Well, I don't know. Someone sleazy, I guess—What's that? You still think he wanted me to know? What is it with you? . . . You're stubborn. All right, I guess I'll have to tell you the truth. It makes me ashamed, but never mind, I've gone this far. . . . You suspected I was lying? Well, you were right. Yes, I wanted to spy on his cell phone. And, as he always kept it on him, I had to be cunning. It wasn't easy, but I did it. I'm kind of nosy, like most women. I thought he'd been acting a little strange lately—Why? I don't know, exactly—Had he changed his aftershave? Yes, he had, actually! Bought a new suit? How did you know? Coming home late at night? Whistling in the shower? Spending all his time checking his texts and hiding himself away to read them? Do you know him, or something? I'm impressed, madame. . . . Oh, the same thing happened to you? Really? Oh yeah? And what did

you do, when you found out he was cheating on you? . . .
You left him! I would love to leave him, madame, but where
would I go? I don't want to go back to my parents' house,
with my little girl. . . . You did that? Oh! If I don't leave
him, he'll start again? Ah . . . So you really think I have to
leave? . . . Uh-huh. And I have to tell him that I know? No
woman should ever stay with an unfaithful husband—is
that what you're saying? But you also said that all husbands
are unfaithful, so why are there any couples who are still
together? That must mean there are women who accept
the infidelity and stay with their husbands. They close their
eyes, or at least they don't go through their husbands'
things, they don't read the texts on their husbands' cell
phones, they don't ask questions if they change the brand of
aftershave they use or if they buy new suits or come home
late or whistle in the shower. You think we have a choice
when we find out we're being cheated on? Either you get
the hell out, or you shut up and put up with it? You would
advise me to get the hell out? Without even talking to him
about it? I just grab my daughter and leave? I don't even say
to him, 'Who's this Lili?' Because I want to know who Lili
is, madame! I refuse to let this Lili steal my husband! That
husband of mine is important to me! Maybe you were
happy to get rid of your husband: maybe he smelled bad or
he snored or he beat you, I don't know, but it's not like that
for me. Gustave and I have been married for four years, and
he can be a very kind and devoted man— You think there
will be other Lilis? Excuse me for saying this, madame,
but I find you depressingly pessimistic! You're against

marriage? Yes, I thought so. You must despise men—I can sense it. So, in your opinion, if some poor guy has a brief fling with a waitress or a receptionist, we should dump him on the spot? So a wife who finds ridiculous texts, full of clichés and spelling mistakes, on her husband's cell phone, should just pack up and leave? Well, good for you, madame! I wish you luck in your narrow, boring little life. I bet you look like an old maid and you live with some mangy cat and spend your evenings watching reality TV shows! Oh, you think that's funny? Go ahead and laugh. I would much rather be an understanding wife than a liberated woman. Good night, madame."

THE "BABY MONITOR"

I do not wish to love anyone,
    for I have no faith in my faithfulness.
    —LOUISE DE VILMORIN (1902–1969), *Notebooks*

Standing in the child-care aisle, Louise was sweating. Her distended belly felt heavy. Inside, she felt the movement of vigorous little fists. She was attempting to decipher the user's guide to a device she had heard great things about. With one hand, she tenderly patted her rounded uterus; in the other, she held that marvel of technical progress, a "Baby Monitor."

A saleswoman, taking pity on Louise's swollen ankles, came toward her.

"Can I help you, madame?"

Louise gave her the grateful smile of a first-time mother.

"Yes, thank you. I've heard a lot about this device, and I'd like to understand how it works."

The woman launched into a sales pitch that would have delighted her department head.

"With the 'Baby Monitor,' you can wave good-bye to all your worries! Your baby—and I can see that the little darling will be with us soon!" she added, with a simper. "Your baby will never go unmonitored; you will be able to hear even the slightest breath, or the quietest sigh."

"How does it work?"

"The 'Baby Monitor' consists of two parts: a transmitter, which you place near your child's crib, and a receiver."

"So it's a bit like a walkie-talkie?"

"Yes, but the difference is that communication is only one-way, so your child won't be woken by any noises around the receiver."

"So I can hear my baby, but my baby can't hear me?"

"Exactly. In this way, you can speak as loud as you like without fear of upsetting your baby, and at the same time you can check how the baby is sleeping, giving you perfect peace of mind. This sophisticated sensor is only triggered when there is a noise. Otherwise, it remains on standby. So you can leave the transmitter on all the time, and switch on the receiver whenever you wish."

"That does sound practical. Does it take batteries?"

"Nine-volt batteries. But both parts can also be plugged into an electrical socket."

"How far does it transmit?"

"Fifty meters."

"I'll take one."

"Excellent choice, madame. I'm sure you'll find it extremely practical when your baby arrives. Do you know if it's a girl or a boy?"

Louise smiled.

"Yes, it's a girl. Her name is Rosie."

ᴥᴥᴥ

Rosie was born a few days later. Back at home, she slept in her crib in a delightfully girly lilac-colored bedroom. And with the "Baby Monitor" Louise could hear every cry and whimper Rosie made.

"What the hell is that?" asked Louise's husband, André, rendered rather surly by the night feeds and the way his life had been turned upside down by the arrival of this bawling, insatiable being.

"It's so I can listen to Rosie no matter where I am. It's really practical. I can go down to see your mother on the first floor. I can even go across the road to buy bread."

A staticky sound came through the receiver, followed by a quivering cry of hunger.

"Oh, our little angel wants more milk!" sang Louise.

"Ugh, how do you unplug this thing?" André sighed.

ᴥᴥᴥ

She could attach the receiver to her belt. Louise never tired of hearing that light, fragile breathing, all those sweet little baby sounds.

At the other end of the apartment, far from the mauve

bedroom, she held the receiver to her ear and listened to her daughter breathe. Terrified, like all mothers, by the thought of Sudden Infant Death Syndrome, Louise kept the device under her pillow at night, the volume turned to its lowest setting. Her husband was oblivious to this fact. Sometimes, when the silence seemed too loud, she would get up in a state of dread and tiptoe to Rosie's room to check that she was still breathing. Then Louise would return to bed, reassured by the little start her baby made when she stroked her cheek.

~❧~

"I still think you should try to lose some weight," said Julietta, Louise's best friend.

Julietta was tall and slim. You would never have guessed she'd had two children.

Three months after Rosie's birth, however, Louise's ankles were still swollen.

Louise shrugged. "I know, I know. André tells me that every day. But I don't have the energy to start a diet."

"You should do it before it's too late."

"Too late?"

"The longer you leave it, the harder it gets. You're nearly thirty, Louise. Be careful."

"Oh, give me a break."

"I'm saying this for your own good. And anyway, think about André."

"What about André?"

"Well, he probably wants his wife back. You were slender, before Rosie."

"I know."

"Men are fragile after a birth. My husband became depressed after our second child. It was him, not me, who got the famous baby blues! And my cousin's husband kept cheating on her after the birth of their son."

"André would never cheat on me."

"How can you be so sure?"

"He has too much respect for me. He puts me on a pedestal. He would never do that."

"I admire your confidence, but I don't think any woman can really be certain of that."

"Did yours cheat on you?"

"I hope not. But to be perfectly honest, I have no idea."

"How would you react if he did?"

"I'd be devastated. Crushed."

Rosie screamed through the receiver.

"She's always hungry, your daughter," Julietta observed.

Louise struggled to her feet and began walking toward the baby's bedroom.

"You're right, Julietta. I need to lose ten pounds."

"More like twenty," said Julietta.

"I hate you."

"I'm the only one who can tell you the truth."

❦

Louise often went down from her fourth-floor apartment to see her mother-in-law on the first floor. The sexagenarian was very fond of her son's wife.

"I'm going to start a diet," Louise told her.

"That's a good idea."

"Oh, am I really that fat?"

"No, my love. Just a little plump. It's normal, after you've had a baby."

"But I've put on over fifty pounds!"

"It happens. I put on sixty when I was pregnant with André. But I lost it all afterward."

"Can I leave the 'Baby Monitor' with you? I have to go to the butcher's, and the reception doesn't work when it's that far away."

"Of course, Louise. Go ahead. I'll keep an eye on Rosie. Or an ear, rather."

⚜

One month later, Louise had lost ten pounds.

"How do I look?" she asked André.

He examined her.

"Fine."

"Notice any difference?"

"No."

Her face fell. "I've lost ten pounds, and you can't even tell?"

"Try to lose a little more."

Louise froze. "You think I'm fat?"

"No, I didn't say that—"

"You just told me I should lose more weight."

"Well, it's true, you are a bit heavier than before the pregnancy. Just lose a few more pounds and you'll be perfect."

"Are you and Julietta in on this together?" Suddenly Louise was filled with rage. "I hate you both! What right does Julietta have to talk to you about my weight? This is crazy!"

She burst into tears.

"Loulou, calm down. You're too on edge these days. It's not good for you."

"I'm on edge because I'm not eating enough." Louise wept.

André took her in his arms and stroked her hair.

"Come on, Loulou, be brave. Think of our baby. And try to eat properly."

Louise sniffed, then calmed down.

"André, have you ever cheated on me?"

André took a step back. "No, of course not! What on earth made you ask me that?"

She shrugged. "Just wondering."

༒

Louise got on the scale. One hundred and fifteen pounds. She sighed with relief. Only a couple more pounds to go and she would be back to her pre-Rosie weight. She was sick to death of this diet. She was slim again, but she felt so strange, angry, lethargic. Dark thoughts filled her head during the day, and at night she had violent, bloody dreams.

The telephone rang. It was Julietta.

"I'm thin again. Well, almost."

"Congrats! I want to come and see. Will you be home in an hour?"

"Let's go out for lunch. Rosie's in day care today. What about Japanese? That's not too fattening."

"Sounds great. Can you book us a table for one o'clock?"

"Okay. I'll go grocery shopping first. We can meet at the restaurant."

Louise hung up. The phone rang again. This time, it was André.

"I've lost my phone charger! I've looked everywhere—it's not in my office."

"It must be here. Let me check."

She looked in their bedroom.

"It's on the bedside table."

"I'll come and pick it up around noon. Will you be home?"

"No. Rosie's in day care until five, so I'm going shopping and then eating lunch with Julietta."

"All right. See you tonight, then."

Louise hung up. She was getting ready to go out when the phone rang for a third time. It was the day-care center: Rosie had a fever and she wouldn't stop crying. Louise had to go fetch her.

After giving her lunch, Louise went down to the first floor with the baby to see Madame Verrières.

"Could you look after Rosie while I go out for lunch? They wouldn't let her stay in day care because she has a slight fever. I've booked a table at the Japanese restaurant for me and Julia. I'll take Rosie to the doctor in the afternoon."

"Of course! Don't worry, Loulou, I'll take care of our little darling. Go eat lunch with your friend. When Rosie gets tired, I'll take her up to her crib. And make sure you eat plenty—you're looking a little thin to me! Give me the 'Baby Phone' and your apartment key."

"Damn it, the light's not working. The batteries must be dead! What time is it?"

"Half past twelve."

"Okay, I'm going across the road to buy batteries. I'll be back in a couple of minutes. Here, take Rosie. . . ."

❧

A few minutes later, with the new batteries installed, the red light shone brightly again. Louise turned the volume to its highest setting.

"I'm turning the sound up, because I've had to move the transmitter further away from her crib, near the hallway. She kept grabbing hold of it, the little devil! It's hidden behind a chair now, so she can't see it."

"Louise, you're going to be late."

Madame Verrières took the receiver from her daughter-in-law.

"Good-bye, my little Rosinette—see you later!" Louise chirped.

Suddenly the receiver emitted a bestial grunting noise.

"Did you hear that?" Louise asked.

"Yes. Very strange."

Louise took the receiver from her mother-in-law and examined it.

There was another grunt, followed by a sensual sigh. Then a woman's voice said, *"Oh yes, that's good! That feels so good! Yes! Yes! Yes!"*

Louise and her mother-in-law were frozen to the spot.

"What is that?" Louise muttered.

"Yes, again! Yes! Yes! Do it again! Oh, it's so good!"

"It sounds like two people making love," whispered the old lady, embarrassed.

Louise listened, in a trance.

A man's voice made them both jump.

"That's how you like it, isn't it? Huh? Tell me!"

"Yes!" the woman bleated. *"Yes, fuck me hard!"*

"Louise, I don't want to listen to those people anymore," mumbled Madame Verrières, who was blushing. "Please, switch it off."

"Fuck you hard? Oh yeah, I'll fuck you hard. You like that, don't you?"

"Oh yes, yes, yes!"

"Louise, switch it off! This is horrible. Please!"

But Louise did not respond. Her thinned-down face was deathly pale.

"It turns you on to do it standing up in the hallway, doesn't it? To do it in our home when Louise is away! You little slut!"

"Oh my God!" breathed Madame Verrières.

Louise looked at her without a word. "It's Julietta and

André," she said in a flat voice, while the couple three floors above groaned with pleasure.

She switched it off.

Silence.

"My poor d-dear . . . ," her mother-in-law stammered.

"Wait here," Louise told her. "I'll be back in five minutes to get Rosie."

"Louise, where are you going?"

Face blank, Louise opened the door. She climbed the stairs quickly and jerkily, like a robot. Her eyes shone.

"Louise, what are you doing?"

Rosie, frightened by her grandmother's anguished voice and by her mother's white face, began to whine.

Madame Verrières could now see nothing of her daughter-in-law but her hand on the bannister.

"Louise! Answer me! You're scaring me."

The hand kept moving smoothly up the bannister, imperturbable.

"Don't worry," Louise called out in a voice that sounded almost normal. "I feel perfectly fine. To tell the truth, I'm starving. I was really looking forward to that sushi. It's a shame, really. I won't be able to have lunch with Julietta because I'm going to kill her."

"Louise! Have you lost your mind?"

Louise was now on the fourth floor. She leaned over the bannister and saw her mother-in-law, petrified, three floors below, the crying baby in her arms.

Louise gave her a pale smile that looked more like a grimace of pain.

"It won't take long, with my meat cleaver. Don't worry—I'll spare André. See you in a minute!"

Then she opened the front door of the apartment, walked inside, and closed it soundlessly behind her.

THE RED NOTEBOOK

The man who loves normally under the sun
adores feverishly under the moon.
—GUY DE MAUPASSANT (1850–1893), *On Water*

MAY 2

Guy is irreproachable. He is deathly dull. The only thing to be done is to cheat on him, a course of action I have been pursuing for quite some time now. I dream of a husband who's a lady-killer, a heartbreaker, a womanizer, a skirt chaser, a charming Casanova, a beautiful bastard! Alas!

I share a sterilized bed with a faithful man. I am married to an easygoing family man who takes me gently, paternalistically, whispering words into my ear that are more tender than exciting, kissing me in a way that is more respectful than earthshaking. To reach nirvana, I must sink into some bawdy vision of lust and debauchery, a delicious dream of sinful violence, complex positions, and coarse language.

MAY 21

My husband bores me.

It's sad but true.

My children are beautiful, but they have never awoken any maternal instinct. I love them, of course, but it's the nanny who brings them up. The idea of taking care of baby bottles, diapers, vaccinations, and walks in the park is utterly foreign to me.

I cheated on him for the first time one month after my wedding, with an ex. I told myself that didn't count, as it wasn't new.

Then I realized it was the only thing that did count.

I soon had to face facts. Cheating on a husband who suspects nothing is almost as boring as not cheating on him at all.

JUNE 4

I have been unfaithful for five years now. Everyone knows, except him. He is ridiculous. If only he would insult me or do the same thing in return!

If only I could find him in bed with my sister or my best

friend or the cleaning lady or even his cousin, his niece, his goddaughter . . . what joy! What a gloriously ridiculed spouse I would be! What insufferable scenes I would make, followed by thrilling reunions in bed. . . .

Alas, the aforementioned conjugal bed has been unrumpled forever! And I am nothing more than a bourgeois wife who is bored with her goody-two-shoes husband, and who—at thirty-two years old—already has one foot in the grave.

JULY 11

I choose my lovers with subtlety and skill. They are rarely part of my circle. Besides, all these devoted dads make me want to scream. They are always in a rush, looking at their watches. I prefer young, firm-fleshed bucks who would rather surrender to my experience than try to get on top (in every sense), as their elders do. Why does Guy never suspect anything? I force myself to leave clues, just to pique his curiosity. But when he finds a man's sock that is not his own at the foot of the bed, he just smiles and puts it aside.

There is nothing more stupid in this world than a faithful husband.

And, as a rule, faithful husbands don't even exist. Guy is a freak of nature. The blood that crawls through his veins must be from some dynasty extinguished by a lack of passion, or impoverished by years of unimaginative inbreeding.

AUGUST 28

All the same, he's not dumb. Poor Guy is simply faithful.

Ever since we were married, I have been devising Machiavellian stratagems to make him cheat on me at last.

I have recruited the most beautiful women and gotten them, without any attempt at delicacy, to sprawl naked at his feet.

In vain. He showed them all his wedding ring as if he were brandishing a crucifix at a bloodthirsty vampire.

So I have had to resign myself. Guy will never cheat on me. It is just not part of his genetic makeup.

SEPTEMBER 3

There is nothing more soporific than a faithful husband, especially when he is yours.

When he falls asleep in the evening after performing his conjugal duties and murmurs, "Sweet dreams, darling," the night—still so young!—stretches out flatly in front of me like the Dead Sea, or an arid tundra without any surprises, any protuberances or hidden crevices.

A husband who never strays is a mediocre husband. What a marriage needs is an unfaithful man to spice it up! A sly, cheating husband exudes sinfulness, oozes lasciviousness, breathes concupiscence. When you lie in bed next to him, you think of the libertine debaucheries of his day, of those other women he has brought to orgasm, and you listen in a blissful state to the convoluted lies he reels off so ingeniously.

Who could ever be bored with an adulterous husband?

OCTOBER 10

Why do I write in this notebook? To palliate my boredom. It never leaves my side. It is secured with a tiny padlock, and I keep the key in a safe hiding place. No one will ever read it. One day, I will burn it.

NOVEMBER 17

Guy has asked me to look for a new apartment, as our rental agreement will not be renewed. I have to find a pleasant four-room residence in a quiet area.

DECEMBER 1

Moving was exhausting. It took me a long time to work up the courage to unpack those final boxes. They were just piled up in the entrance hall.

Then, one rainy day when the children were at school and I wasn't expecting anyone, I finally decided to put them away. Inside I found a bunch of old papers: payment slips, accounts, old photographs, road maps, leaflets—the kind of junk you amass over the years.

I feel too tired. Or not brave enough. I will finish this entry later.

DECEMBER 18

I found a nice café, where I like to come and read newspapers, and write. I must continue my story. It's raining outside.

So, those old papers . . .

I went through them, tossing anything that seemed useless, putting aside whatever we might still need. It was a notebook—a bit like mine, only red, and larger, and without a padlock. I had never seen it before. I opened it. Inside were women's names, with dates and places. It was all in Guy's handwriting. For example, I read:

> Paris, Winter '98:
> Laure
> Yvette
> the Rondoli sisters
>
> Étretat, Spring 2000:
> Fifi
> Ludivine
> Harriet

Fécamp, June 2002:
Adrienne L.

Then there were remarks, some with spelling mistakes (that I will not reproduce), such as:

Côte d'Azur, Summer 2004:
Hermine (aka The Spitter)
Rosalie (nice)
Adélaide (too fat)
Lise (crap)

I kept turning the pages, reading the lists of names. I wasn't mentioned. This annoyed me.

I'm going to order another coffee.

DECEMBER 20

I have to finish this story.

I have to talk about the other women's names—those that came after we were married. Their names mean nothing to me. All I know is that he had them in Paris, mostly during my pregnancies, then occasionally after that. For the past year, however, the pages of the red notebook show only mysterious initials without dates, places, or comments.

It doesn't bother me to discover he's had mistresses. On the contrary, it is reassuring.

What bothers me is thinking that Guy no longer loves me. In fact, I don't think he ever loved me.

The mask of the simpleton has slipped. Now I see Guy's true face. And that face suddenly strikes me as magnificent.

DECEMBER 24

Dear Jeanne,

I imagine you are rather startled to see my handwriting in your private diary.

So, you've found it at last—my red notebook! And I have finally unlocked yours. God knows I left that notebook in plain sight for years. Yet you never noticed it. I wanted to see how far your effrontery and your vanity would take you. You imagined yourself the only one capable of cheating and lying. And you took an exquisite pleasure in it. It was amusing. For five years, I enjoyed playing the gullible husband, the honorable spouse, the cuckold who closes his eyes. But, as I'm sure you realize, my dear Jeanne, that can't last forever.

Not once did it enter your head that I, too, might be cheating. Not once did you suspect me. You found it priceless to make your husband look like an imbecile. Oh, my poor Jeanne. What will become of you now? And your young men? Are you so tempting to them now? On whom will you cheat? To whom will you tell your lies?

I can imagine you, frozen with shock, as you read these pages, in that café where you've spent so much time recently. And the worst thing must be that you are now realizing that you love me. I can see it from here—the light of love finally softening your sharp features, like the sun rising for the first time.

I am going to leave you now, my dear Jeanne, not only at the foot of this page, but forever— because I have nothing else to say to you.

You no longer amuse me. Frankly, you bore me. May God bless you this Christmas.

But look on the bright side—you were right all along! There is no such thing as a faithful husband.

Guy

The Answering Machine

Unable to suppress love,
the Church wanted at least to disinfect it,
so it created marriage.
> —CHARLES BAUDELAIRE (1821–1867),
> *My Heart Laid Bare*

APRIL 1992

Someone must have been playing with the answering machine again—it's flashing!'

"What?"

"Look, it's broken. We've only had it one day and it's already broken."

"You pressed the wrong button."

Charles leaned over the machine.

"There you go. See? All fixed."

Lola shrugged. "I don't like it—it's too complicated. I'll never use it."

"Just ask your sons. They'll explain it to you."

She looked at the little brown box.

"I must be turning into an old fogey. I hate these machines. I don't like leaving messages on them or listening to the messages other people leave me. I never know which button to press."

"This one's really cool, too," said ten-year-old Sébastien. "There's a voice that tells you the exact day and time when the message was left, because most people forget to say that, and it doesn't bother recording if there's no message!"

"What do you mean?" asked Lola. "So what does it do if someone hangs up without leaving a message?"

"Well, it doesn't record that horrible beeping noise. It doesn't even show up as a message. If someone hangs up, the machine just ignores it."

"And you can check your messages from outside the house, too!" added eleven-year-old Benjamin.

"Incredible," Lola said sarcastically.

"You should learn how to use it," said Benjamin, "instead of making stupid criticisms."

"Answering machines are very practical," Sébastien declared.

Just then, the telephone rang and the whole family stood up.

"Let's test it. Everyone in position!" Charles ordered, excited as a kid.

All eyes were on the brown box. At the third ring, Charles's deep voice boomed across the room: "Hello! You've reached forty-eighty-nine-thirty-four-fifty-six. Please leave a message for Lola, Sébastien, Benjamin, or Charles and they'll call you back. Begin speaking after you hear the beep. Thanks. Talk to you soon."

"Your message is too long," Lola said.

"Shush! Listen!"

"Hello, this is Alexandre for Benjamin. He can call me back whenever. Good-bye."

A complex mechanical clinking noise followed, and then a strange metallic voice announced: "Saturday, six thirty-three pm."

"Amazing, isn't it?" said Charles. "Look, darling, I'll show you how to listen to this message. It's perfectly simple. Imagine you've just come home and you see that the light is flashing. That means there's a message. To listen to it, you just press here. Try it."

She pressed the button, and Alexandre's message was played again, followed by the metallic voice.

"Now that you know Alexandre has called, you have two possibilities. You could delete the message, but as it's for Benjamin, you probably shouldn't."

"You'd better not!" grumbled the eleven-year-old.

"So you leave it the way it is until Benjamin hears the message and deletes it himself. But let's pretend this message was from . . . I don't know, Sylvie, say, or one of your other friends. . . ."

"Fanny!" simpered Benjamin, hand on hip.

"Caroline!" sang Sébastien, prancing around the room.

"Stop it, boys! You're being idiotic."

"Anyway," Charles said, "so let's say there's a message for

you. You listen to it by pressing this button; then afterward you delete it, like this. May I?" he asked Benjamin, who nodded.

Charles pressed another button and they heard the shrill sound of the message being rewound.

"And that's it. Gone! Easy, isn't it?"

"There's something else you should explain to Mom," said Sébastien. "If you pick up the phone as the answering machine starts working, because you've forgotten to switch it off, it records your conversation. And that uses up the cassette. So you must remember to delete it afterward."

"Very good point." Charles nodded approvingly. "You understand, darling?"

"I think so."

"You'll see—this answering machine is going to change your life!"

❧

Later, Lola said to her husband, "Do you think I'm stupid because I don't know how to use the answering machine?"

He looked at her, surprised. "What? Of course not, Lola!"

"I feel like you think I'm stupid."

"What are you talking about?"

"I feel old and ugly."

"You're thirty-three!"

"And you can tell."

"Don't be ridiculous. You're a beautiful woman, and you know it."

❦

The next day, when she returned home from the grocery store, she noticed that the light on the answering machine was red. She put down her bags and knelt next to the machine. Frowning with concentration, she pressed the button. One message for Benjamin, another for Sébastien. She felt disappointed, but at least she had managed to work the thing properly! While she was unpacking her bags in the kitchen, the telephone rang. Standing on a stool so she could arrange the jars of jam on a shelf, she allowed herself the luxury of letting the machine answer for her.

It was Charles.

"Darling, it's me. I'll be leaving later for that presentation in Brussels. Don't wait up for me this evening—I might have to spend the night there. If you need to get ahold of me, Nicole has the phone number. Bye, darling. I love you!"

Lola sighed as she got down from the stool. Charles was often away from home. At thirty-four he had been given a big promotion in the advertising agency where he worked, and for the last two years he had rarely spent a whole week at home. Lola had done her best to get used to his absences. The boys had their own lives, their friends, school. But it seemed to her that she no longer had anything. The days stretched out emptily before her, flat, smooth, and featureless. She should have gone back to work after Sébastien was born, but she had chosen to stay at home and look after her children. And for eight years, that had been fulfilling.

The boys were older now, though, and they no longer needed her. She was bored. Most of all, she was afraid of becoming boring. Charles seemed happy with her, but was he really? Maybe she should have that third child—the little girl they had dreamed of. It wasn't too late.

Lola nestled on the sofa and lit a cigarette, her eyes dreamy. The phone rang again. She did not move, and the machine picked up.

"Hey there, sweetie—it's Fanny. I love your new answering machine! You want to go see a movie this afternoon? Call me. Bye!"

Lola didn't feel like calling Fanny, whose enthusiasm for life sometimes irritated her. She knelt next to the answering machine in order to delete the last two messages. The machine obeyed her orders. Charles would be happy! Her face clouded over. Why did she always think about Charles's reaction? Why did she always force herself to behave properly for him, like a pupil with a teacher? Irritated, she lit another cigarette and decided to bake an apple pie for the boys. And the day went on, long and colorless, until she was rescued by the arrival of her sons.

✤

Charles was gone most of the week. A few days after his return, Lola received a phone call from her mother, who lived alone in Honfleur. She wanted to see her daughter and her grandsons.

"Take the boys to Normandy for the weekend," Charles told Lola. "The fresh air will do them good, and you'll get some rest."

"I'm not tired," she protested.

"You are, darling. You have bags under your eyes."

She blushed.

"That's because you kept me from sleeping most of the night."

He embraced her, stroking her rump affectionately.

"I missed you. . . ."

Charles had rarely ever been so attentive. Since he came back from Brussels, they had made love with more ardor than usual.

"Will you come to Mom's, too?"

He knotted his tie. "I don't think I'll be able to, honey. I'd like to take advantage of the apartment being empty to get some work done and get my files in order. I'm sure you understand. . . ."

"I do, but it's a shame. The boys see so little of you. And as for Mom—"

"You'll be able to explain it to her, darling, I know you will. But I have to go. See you tonight. Don't expect me for dinner, though."

He slipped out. She sighed, then started making the bed, which they had made quite a mess of. If Charles were that loving every time he came back from a trip, life wouldn't be so bad.

She spent the weekend at her mother's house, with her boys. On Saturday, about 11:00 P.M., she called Charles. The answering machine picked up. Not knowing what to say, she hung up. So where was he at 11:00 on a Saturday night? Maybe he was working and he'd put the answering machine on in order to not be disturbed? She called him back and left a message that she thought sounded garbled and clumsy. The next day, she tried again about 9:00 am, and then again at noon. Each time, she got the answering machine and the recording of Charles's cheerful voice. She didn't leave a message. Around 5:00 pm, as she was about to depart with her children, Charles called.

"Where were you all weekend?" she asked irritably.

"Here, honestly! I was working!"

"I kept getting the answering machine."

"I told you I wanted to work in peace."

"But I don't understand. I called you several times—"

"I got your message last night, after I'd finished work, but it was too late to call you back. I didn't want to wake your mother. Are you coming home now?"

"Yeah, we're on our way," she said, feeling suddenly weary.

⁓✢⁓

Another week passed, then two more, monotonous. Lola was pale; she felt numb, lifeless. Her friend Fanny suggested Lola get checked out professionally. She booked an appointment with her family doctor, but he found nothing alarming. He prescribed some blood tests and a urine sample.

"You might be slightly anemic. I'll call you tomorrow if I find anything abnormal. In the meantime, get some rest."

◈

The next day, returning home in the late afternoon, she saw there was a message on the answering machine. It was from her friend Caroline. Lola halfheartedly listened to it, then pressed the delete button. The cassette rewound for a long time. She stood up to light a cigarette. Suddenly the machine made a strange, staticky noise.

"Damn, I must have gotten the wrong button!"

She pressed a different switch, then another. The crackling ended, but the cassette kept playing. She didn't know how to stop it. She tried every button on the machine.

"Oh shit!"

She could already imagine the exasperated look on Charles's face.

Suddenly she heard raised voices. After a moment or two, she recognized one of them as Charles's.

"Please, Apollonie, calm down!"

Lola froze. Then she moved closer to the machine.

A young woman's voice—firm sounding and completely unknown to Lola—filled the room.

"How am I supposed to calm down, Charles?"

"Please try, Apollonie. There's no point working yourself into a state about it."

Lola felt puzzled. Then she realized Charles must have grabbed the phone just as the answering machine clicked into action. It had recorded a conversation between her husband and this stranger, this Apollonie.

Lola pressed the pause button, and the cassette stopped. Did she want to hear what came next? Wouldn't it be better to erase the whole thing, to pretend she had never heard those voices, to close her eyes, protect herself? Charles probably thought he'd deleted this conversation. He must have done something wrong, erased only part of it.

After a few seconds of hesitation, Lola released the pause button and the cassette kept playing.

"For the past year, you've been promising to leave your wife, going on and on about how bored to death you are with her, how your kids drive you nuts, how your family sucks, and how you want to feel young again!"

"Apollonie, listen—"

"No, Charles, I've had it! You know perfectly well I can give you that second youth, but you don't have the balls to leave your wife. That's all there is to it—you're a coward!"

"Listen to me. They'll be home soon."

"Then don't forget to unmake your bed and eat whatever your old lady left for you in the fridge. Otherwise she'll realize you weren't home all weekend."

"I'll call you later. See you at one tomorrow, okay? Have you calmed down?"

"Do you love me?"

"Of course I do, but stop acting like a spoiled brat, will

you? I can't just drop everything for you. My wife wouldn't bear it. She needs me. I'm everything for her. And my sons are still young. It would be terrible to leave them now. They'd hate me for the rest of their lives. Just give me some time, sweetie, okay?"

"Okay, okay! But I'm warning you: I'm not going to wait ten years. Ten years from now, I'll be your wife's age and you won't want me anymore."

Charles laughed.

"I will always want you, and your divine body. . . . See you tomorrow, babe. Rue du Dôme, okay?'

Apollonie blew him a loud kiss and they hung up.

"Sunday, six fifteen pm," the metallic voice announced.

Before Lola could react, the telephone rang again. Devastated by what she had heard, she just sat there, frozen.

The answering machine took over. After the beep, her doctor's voice was heard.

"Hello, this is Dr Aupick. I have some wonderful news for you, confirmed by the blood tests. You're pregnant, madame! So please book an appointment with your obstetrician. Congratulations. I'll send you the results of the blood tests. Good-bye."

"Thursday, three thirty-seven pm."

Lola was too shocked to move a muscle. Her breathing came in fits and starts, mouth open, as if she'd just been punched in the stomach.

Then, very quickly, without thinking, she pressed the delete button. A swirl of noise as the messages rewound.

She checked that the cassette tape was blank again. Apollonie, Charles, and Dr Aupick had all vanished.

Lola took a deep breath and got to her feet. She touched her flat stomach. Inside her, a baby was growing. She smiled. It was a girl; she was sure of it.

The Au Pair Girl

What greater pleasure
than to cheat the cheater!
—Jean de La Fontaine (1621–1695),
"The Cock and the Fox"

On the top floor of a fancy store in Rue de Passy, two young women were eating a light lunch of Château-Thierry pie and Vaux-le-Vicomte salad. The restaurant's windows overlooked the gray rooftops of Paris and the atmosphere was so hushed and refined that they might have been in England.

One of the women was blond, with a pale, delicate complexion and light blue eyes. She wore a lapis-lazuli jacket, braided with bister silk, with round golden buttons that matched her earrings. Her hair was smoothed back in a ponytail, exposing a childlike forehead with barely a wrinkle. Her white fingers looked too fragile to be sporting a round diamond (on her left ring finger) and a heavy gold signet ring (on her right pinkie).

The other young woman wore a leather redingote over an ivory-colored blouse. Her golden-brown hair framed a slightly lined and very expressive face with hazel eyes, high cheekbones, and thin red lips. Her hands were squarish, her fingernails cut short, and no rings shone on any of her fingers.

Marguerite, the blonde, worked as a publicist for a high-street fashion house. Marie, the brunette, was an advertising executive for a weekly women's magazine. They ate lunch together once a month for professional reasons, but always enjoyed each other's company.

An elegant older woman sat down at a neighboring table. She gave them a friendly smile, then took out her cell phone while she waited for her guest. Marguerite and Marie smiled politely in return.

"Did you notice?" Marie whispered.

"Yes. She's had a face-lift," Marguerite replied quietly.

"Not a success, if you ask me."

"Hideous."

"Don't look now, but Marie-Hélène has just walked in carrying the same purse as yours."

Marguerite shot a quick glance across the room, then lifted a disdainful eyebrow.

"It's a fake. That color doesn't exist. She must have ordered it in Place du Palais-Bourbon, from that guy who does pretty good imitations."

Marie leaned over her tablet, her index finger scrolling impatiently down a page of photographs.

"So, where were we?"

"I was telling you about the perfume launch."

"Oh yes. So this is what I propose. . . ."

Marguerite listened, but her thoughts were clearly elsewhere. She looked wearily out the window.

Marie stared at her. "What's the matter?"

Marguerite ordered their coffees and played distractedly with a spoon.

"I'm exhausted."

"Yes, you look tired."

"I am."

"Too much work?"

"No more than usual."

Marie drank her coffee. Marguerite did not touch hers.

Then she said, "I'm not sure if I should tell you this. . . . We're not close friends, after all. . . ."

"Sometimes it's easier to confide in someone you don't know that well."

"That's true."

Silence.

"You can tell me if you want."

Marguerite hesitated.

"Yes, I would like that. I'm too ashamed to admit this to my closest friends."

"I'm guessing it's about your husband?"

"Exactly."

Marguerite had turned red. She looked down for a moment, then confronted Marie's dark gaze.

"Promise me you'll keep this to yourself."

"Of course, darling. I swear on my daughter's head."

Again Marguerite hesitated. She drank her tepid coffee, then looked around at the chattering bourgeois customers, the bustling waitresses, the endless procession of well-dressed women. For the first time, she noticed that there were no men in this restaurant. It was a feminine cocoon, a gynaeceum, where women came to talk about men.

As her friend wavered, Marie leaned in close and whispered: "Has your husband been a bad boy?"

Marguerite turned her azure eyes away. "Yes."

"What did he do?"

Finally, Marguerite met her eyes. "Jean is cheating on me."

"He's cheating on you?"

"Keep your voice down. People are looking at us," Marguerite said coldly. "Yes, Jean is cheating on me."

"How do you know?"

Marguerite ordered another coffee. "I know."

"Have you found any clues?"

Marguerite snickered, revealing her tiny white incisors. "I saw him."

Marie sat up. "You saw him cheating on you?"

"Yes."

"Oh, my darling! How awful."

Silence.

"Who was it?"

"The au pair."

Silence again.

"That's horrible."

"Absolutely horrible," Marguerite agreed.

"Are you sure about this?"

"What else are you supposed to think when you find your husband in bed with the au pair girl?"

"Oh my God!" said Marie. "What are you going to do, my darling?"

Marguerite smiled again. "What am I going to do? Do you really want to know?"

"I would be capable of suicide if my husband did that to me."

"No, I'm not going to kill myself."

"Or I'd become depressed."

"I'm not planning on a depression."

"Then I'd leave him."

"I'm not going to leave him either."

"Because of the children?"

"Of course because of the children. I have a much better idea."

"What?"

"I'm going to cheat on him! And I will tell him all about my affair, without omitting any of the juicy details. I'll make him squirm; I'll make him retch. He'll regret what he did to me for the rest of his life. It will be my supreme revenge."

"An eye for an eye, a tooth for a tooth?"

"Exactly."

"Who will you choose?"

"His best friend, Pierre."

"You're crazy! Your husband will kill you."

Marguerite blushed again, but this time with anger. "Crazy? How would you feel, in my place? Imagine you go home unexpectedly, thinking about something else entirely a photo shoot, or a new collection, or a mailing list—and you walk into your bedroom and you see a vision of horror: your husband in bed with an eighteen-year-old Swedish girl."

Marie shivered. "What's she like, this Swedish girl?"

Marguerite took a drag on her e-cigarette. "Much too sexy. Blond, a gorgeous body. I should never have hired her. But, you know, I honestly thought Jean was above that sort of thing. He's a very busy man. His time is taken up by the bank, the Dow Jones, the CAC 40, his golf weekends, and his polo games. I'm still in shock. Men are beasts, when it comes down to it, don't you think?"

"Oh, absolutely. You should have hired a fat, old, ugly Filipino woman. I could never have rested easily, knowing my husband was alone in the house with the next Scarlett Johansson. You should never tempt a man! Especially not a man in his thirties."

"Apparently it's even worse when they hit fifty." Marguerite sighed. "The midlife crisis, you know? My husband seems to have started a little early. . . ."

"How will you go about it, with his friend Pierre?" Marie asked.

"I'll just get straight to the point. I'll ask him if he wants to sleep with me."

"What if he says no?"

"He won't."

"Have you seduced many men since you got married?"

Stung by this, Marguerite shrugged. "Seducing a man is like riding a bike—you never forget how. Even if you've been married for ten years."

"Have you talked to Jean?"

"He doesn't know that I know. I left the room without making a sound. He didn't see me."

"Were they asleep?"

"No, they were fucking. He was taking her from behind, doggy-style."

"Oh, that's dreadful."

"Yep. In the middle of the morning, in my own bedroom. On my own bed."

"It's despicable. How did you manage to sleep in your bed that night?"

"I didn't."

"So where did you sleep?"

"I'm going to sleep in Pierre's bed, tonight. It happened this morning. Look, I'm all ready." She lifted up an elegant overnight bag.

"Wow. I'm impressed, Marguerite."

"I bet you'd do the same thing, in my position."

"I think I'd have killed the pair of them."

"I must be calmer than you."

"And more Machiavellian. But what if Pierre does say no?"

Marguerite picked up her cell phone and checked it

quickly, put her e-cigarette in its holder, then asked for the check.

"Marie, no man could refuse a woman who gives herself to him, the way I'm going to do with Pierre. He won't resist, even if I am his best friend's wife. In fact, I bet that makes it even more exciting for him."

"And afterward?"

She pulled a face. "We'll see."

"So you've never cheated on Jean before?"

"I should have done. I feel so stupid, so naïve! If only I'd known . . ."

Marie laughed softly. "I've done it."

"You've been unfaithful?"

"Yes. I'd just had my daughter. I was feeling frumpy. It was in Touquet, during the summer holidays. My husband was working in Paris."

"And?"

"There was this young guy—not bad, a bit of a rube—who was coming on to me. I was playing golf with my parents-in-law, and he followed me. I ended up saying yes, because I was bored. We lay down in the rough and had sex, very quickly."

"How was it?"

"Not great. Afterward, I told him my husband was on his way, and that he should leave me alone. I never even knew his name."

"And since then?"

"Since then, I've been faithful. I'm scared of catching AIDS."

"Oh shit!" Marguerite said, dropping her cell phone on the tablecloth.

"What?"

"The rubbers!"

"What about them?"

"I don't have any!"

"So?"

"I can't sleep with Pierre without a rubber, can I?"

"You think your husband wore a rubber, with the Swede?"

"The Swedes use rubbers more than any other national-ity in the world. The Scandinavians are totally pro-condom!"

"Well, just go buy some at the pharmacy."

Marguerite bit her lip. "That's such a nuisance!"

"Why?"

"I'm embarrassed to buy them."

"I'll buy some for you, if you like."

"You won't believe this, but I have no idea how to use them. I've never put a condom on a man in my life."

"Your Pierre will know how. The man usually does it, anyway. It's like putting on a sock. Just don't get it the wrong way round. It's not difficult."

"This messes up my whole plan. How am I supposed to seduce him if I have to put that thing on him?"

"He'll do it himself."

"Yes, but who's supposed to bring up the subject—him or me? How does it happen these days? It's the first time I've been in this kind of situation. And what am I supposed to say, exactly? 'Would you mind wearing a thingamajig . . . you know, a whatsit—' Ugh! It'll turn him off in an instant."

"I wouldn't say anything. I'd just put it on him myself."

"And what if I get it on the wrong way? What if I end up wearing it like a glove and he loses his erection? Oh, what a nightmare!"

"There are different sizes and models, too—"

"No!"

"Oh yes. There's king-size, super king-size, and extra-super king size."

"What does that mean?"

"It means men can't bear the idea of walking into a store and asking for a pack of 'medium'-sized condoms. Then there's lubricated, unlubricated, different flavors—vanilla, pear, banana, strawberry—and different colors. You can get them with patterns or without, with studs or ribs—shall I go on?"

"Where did you learn all this, Marie?"

"I gave up using the pill at one point. Would you like me to come with you, to buy some? I could help you choose."

Marguerite sighed. "Oh . . . no, thank you, darling. I think I'll just go home and beat the crap out of my husband. It's less complicated."

She removed the large gem from the ring finger of her left hand and put it on her right. Now the thick signet ring and the engagement ring were touching. She made a fist and looked at it appraisingly.

"Look—I have brass knuckles now! So that diamond will finally serve some purpose."

"What purpose?"

"If I aim right, I should be able to knock out his dental implant."

The Strand of Hair

It's still better to be married than dead.
—Molière (1622–1673),
Les Fourberies de Scapin

Dear Jean-Baptiste,
Yes, I destroyed everything. There's nothing left. The glassware is in pieces. The porcelain dishes are jigsaw puzzles. The paintings are slashed. The couches disemboweled. The books torn to shreds. Your computer exploded. The TV and the DVD player beyond repair. Your iPad is in the toilet bowl. Your suits have no arms or legs. Your shoes have been soaked in bleach.

I created this mess in quite a methodical way. I wanted to attack everything that represented the eight years we spent together. It hurt me to look at our photograph albums. All those images of vanished happiness, short-lived contentment, all those smiling faces, those family scenes, our honeymoon, our first Christmas together, those birthdays and vacations . . . I couldn't bear to look at them anymore. So I burned them, one by one, along with all your letters.

The CDs and DVDs were more difficult. They're surprisingly hard to break. But I managed in the end, with the aid of a large pair of scissors. I particularly enjoyed destroying *La Wally* and the song that was sung at our wedding: "Ebben? Ne andrò lontana." I don't think I ever want to hear that again.

How did I find out? I bet that's what's bugging you, isn't it? I can imagine it so easily: this letter trembling in your hands, your struggle to stay upright amid the disorder of this disaster zone, this cemetery, this chaos that used to be our apartment, and still what bothers you most is that you can't work out how I discovered the truth.

While you're racking your brains, I would like to tell you a thing or two.

I remember our first meeting vividly. We were twenty-five years old. You were tall, handsome, charming. You smiled at me. It was a crowded party. We talked—all night long. And we saw each other again. And we got married. And then there was Angélique. You wanted a girl. You dreamed of having a daughter. When she was born, you cried. I remember your tears and your big hands protecting her tiny, fragile body. You told me it was the greatest day of your life. Then there was Octave. You weren't so interested in him. He senses that, you know. He's aware of it. He's only four, but he's extraordinarily sensitive. Not that you ever noticed. He realized that you hurt me, even though I was careful not to say anything to the children. He told me he doesn't want you to make me sad anymore. I think he's right. The children are with me. They know nothing.

I came back here, one last time, and I destroyed everything. I bet you didn't think I'd be capable, did you? Your darling wife, so gentle, so kind, so well brought up. The patient mother. The exemplary spouse. No doubt you'll tell the insurance company your apartment was trashed by a gang of vandals. It happens all the time.

I wanted to hurt you by destroying the objects you loved. It felt good. You probably think it was beneath me. But it made me feel better. I look at this mayhem and I breathe more easily. The violence rose within me like an erupting volcano. I let it explode. Now I am calm. The storm is over. I know I never want to live with you again. It was this summer that I realized you were cheating on me. I was in Brittany with the children. You were working in Paris. When I came home after the vacation, I found a long strand of black hair in the bathtub. No one in our family has black hair, apart from you. And yours is short. This strand of hair was at least a foot long. It lay on the white enamel like a dark party streamer. I looked at it, then rinsed the bathtub. I didn't say a word.

A few weeks later, I found another one stuck to your sweater. Long and black. Again, I kept silent. You know me. I'm not the kind of girl to make a scene. I stay in my corner. I watch. I observe. I don't think I've ever yelled at you, have I? For years, I held it all in. What you're looking at now is the result. Sometimes it's dangerous to not yield to anger. Look where it got us.

Then, one day, I left home for a few days on a work trip. Your mother looked after the children. When I came back, I found a long strand of black hair under your pillow. So I did what women do when they are suspicious. I followed you. This required a certain amount of organization. No one becomes a private detective overnight.

I saw you with her. A tall girl with long, dark hair, quite pretty, nice smile, slim but curvy body. You went into a café near your office. It was late afternoon. You looked at her with so much love, so much passion, that I wanted to throw up. You drank in her words; you caressed her hands, her shoulders, her thighs under the table. The two of you shared a sensual kiss. I noticed you weren't wearing your wedding ring. It was at that moment that I decided to leave you.

That evening, when you came home, the wedding ring was on your finger again. Its presence confirmed my plans. Yes, I was going to leave you. Not right away. But soon.

I don't want to hear your explanations. I suppose all betrayed wives must listen to their husbands' excuses, but I choose not to submit myself to yours. As far as I'm concerned, you have no excuse. Coming home in the evening, you transformed yourself from cheating husband to glowing father with an ease that was stunning. You spent hours with the children, especially Angélique, reading her stories, helping her with her homework. You were kind and sweet to me. Tender and affectionate. That is what hurt me—the impudence of your double life, the complacency with which you willingly took on first one role, then the other. You cheated on all three of us—Angélique, Octave, and me. Now it's over. The curtain has dropped, Jean-Baptiste.

I mulled over my departure for a long time. I had to choose the right moment, the perfect opportunity. In the meantime, I found out the name, address, and occupation of your mistress. Armande B., 40 Rue Richelieu, 1st arrondissement. A beautician, working in a salon at 19 Rue Mazarine. I even went into that beauty salon, to buy some lipstick. She was friendly, professional, in her white blouse and impeccably applied makeup. When she turned her back to me, I was gripped with a sudden desire to kill her. There was no one else in the shop. I could have stabbed her in the back, plunged a knife into that spotless white material. No one would have known.

I paid in cash so I wouldn't have to reveal my identity. She never suspected a thing. She was perfectly polite to me. I was tempted to say to her, "I'm Jean-Baptiste's wife. I know everything," just to see the look on her face. But I didn't. I wanted to take my time.

For another two months, I endured your lies, the supposed traffic jams that caused your late arrivals, the last-minute work meetings, the weekends when So-and-So would call you regarding an urgent case. You deployed the full arsenal of the unfaithful husband. I accepted this in silence. I prepared my vengeance. Then came the day when you told me you had to go away for a week for your job. The day after your departure, I called the beauty salon to ask for an appointment with Mademoiselle B. They told me she had taken a week off. So I called the hotel where you were staying. I asked for Armande B. I was informed that no guest was registered under that name. "Oh, how silly of me!" I said in a cheerful voice. "Of course, she's Madame Jean-Baptiste Jourdain now." They told me that Monsieur and Madame Jourdain had gone out. So I knew she was with you.

You called home every evening, talking for a long time to Angélique and then to Octave. It was incredible to think that you were with another woman, that you were sleeping with her, while you said such sweet and tender things to me. It only intensified my desire for revenge.

The day of your return, you came home early, with gifts for the whole family. The children were delighted. That night, you made love to me for a long time. You really applied your-self. I tolerated it in silence. It was horrific. You told me you loved me. I wanted to die.

The next day—yesterday, in other words—I decided the moment had come. I packed the suitcases. First the chil-dren's, then mine. I told them this morning that we were going to move to a new house, but that in the meantime we would be staying at my parents' place. They were very ex-cited. Octave asked me if you were coming, too. I said no, not right away. He cried. I consoled him as best I could. You need to speak to him.

I told my parents that I was leaving you. I didn't explain why. You can tell them whenever you like. I'm going to find an apartment for the three of us. I thank God that I have a job of my own, so I'm not dependent on you. What do housewives do when they want to leave their husbands? I have already started using my maiden name again. It's a relief not to be Madame Jourdain anymore.

One last thing, Jean-Baptiste. Don't try to explain. The only thing I want to talk to you about is divorce. For the rest, it's over. We'll find a solution for the children. One couple in two gets divorced in Paris. We won't be the first. Or the last. We will act in the children's best interests.

I also wanted to say that I couldn't destroy the silverware. In order to cut short any tawdry arguments, I took half of it. So that leaves you twelve knives, forks, spoons, etc. You can also keep the furniture, even the pieces belonging to me. I don't want to see them anymore. On the other hand, I took all the children's things, because I want their lives to change as little as possible.

You will be home soon. I should hurry up and leave. The concierge came up, concerned about the noise. I explained that I'd knocked over a few boxes when I was tidying up the apartment. You can tell him to send on my mail.

Your ex-wife

The Woods

Lamblike lovers become wolfish husbands.
—Isaac de Benserade (1613?–1691), *Poem on Their Majesties' Consummation of Marriage*

It is a cold November evening and a light rain is falling over the woods. Cars move slowly down damp paths, tires hissing on the asphalt, coming and going and coming again, their headlights picking out the leafless trees and the figures who stand on the sidewalk, hips swaying, lips pouting, provocative. Behind a steamed-up window, hungry eyes. A car stops, the window is lowered, the prostitute leans down, and the age-old business of the woods begins again. She utters a few words. The man nods. The prostitute walks around the car, heels tapping the concrete. She opens the passenger door and sits down. Then the car disappears into darkness, in search of a quieter side path.

It is an evening like any other evening in the woods. The rain and the cold do not dampen the desires of these nocturnal prowlers for their regular fix of venal love. She looks at her watch. Eleven thirty. At midnight, she will go home. Another half hour to endure—so, three or four blow jobs, at €20 or €25 apiece. With a little smile, she watches as a metallic blue sedan passes for the fifth time, one of those family cars in which she so often ends up, with a baby seat and boosters for kids in the backseat. From behind the windshield, a man in his early thirties looks out at her, his expression almost fearful, his jaw clenched. She smiles at him, not too flirtatiously. You have to be careful with first-timers, because they have a tendency to flee. The car stops a little way off. One of her colleagues sets off, breasts exposed in spite of the grim weather. "Stop!" she shouts. "This one's mine." She moves toward the car. The window is lowered. She crouches down. He doesn't know what to say, what to ask for. He clears his throat, but no words emerge. So, in a gentle voice that seems to surprise him, she intones the same words she repeats fifty times a day, a night: "Twenty for a blow job, fifty *pour l'amour.*" He doesn't dare meet her eyes. She knows all too well what her own face must look like at this time of night, in artificial light, after a long, hard day's work. But she also guesses that this man has not come to these bare trees, after his own day at work, in search of beauty and freshness. She knows he will not remember her face. "Blow job." A whisper. She walks around the car, opens the door, sits down. His hands are still gripping the wheel tensely. "Take the second road on the right," she says, in the same gentle voice. He follows her instructions. The car enters a dark pathway. The sky is barely visible between the criss-crossing branches above. She politely asks for her €20. Startled, he searches his pockets, becoming agitated and switching on the ceiling light. She notices he's wearing cordu-roy pants and a parka. Finally, he locates his wallet and re-moves a bill with trembling fingers. As he hands it to her, the wedding ring he wears on his left hand catches the light and shines brightly. Hurriedly he switches off the ceiling light. She asks him to unzip his pants, and he does. She bends down over this stranger's penis, the God-knows-how-many-eth of the night. It is not completely hard, so she masturbates it for a while. She hears the man's breathing turn heavy. Fi-nally, he is erect. She opens the condom packet with expert grace and puts it on him. Then she gets to work. She knows the first time is always very quick, and this client proves no exception. A few seconds later the man comes with a sort of strangled groan. She gives him a few seconds to recover, then removes the used condom and puts it in a plastic bag she has brought for that purpose. "There you go," she says. "Did you like it? Was that okay?" He nods, then suddenly begins to sob. "Now, now . . . come on, *chéri,* don't cry. It's always like this, the first time. I bet you feel guilty, don't you? Your wife will never find out. All my clients are married men."

⁕

His wife is preparing the baby's bottle. Her face drawn by the sleepless nights she has endured since the child's birth.

The baby screams impatiently, wriggling in his crib. Stifling a yawn, she warms up the bottle. The baby is choking with rage, his face turning purple. She takes him in her arms and cuddles him. He calms down. She puts a bib around the baby's neck, grabs the bottle, checks the temperature by pouring a few drops onto her wrist, and settles down to feed him. He drinks slowly and greedily, staring up into her bluish eyes. She is almost asleep on her chair, with this hot bundle pressed close against her. All is quiet. She feels tired. The baby burps on her shoulder; she tells him he's a good boy, changes his diaper, and puts him back in his crib, a stuffed animal to one side and a musical box to the other. She winds up the musical box, but he's already falling asleep. So she tiptoes out of the room and goes to take a look at his big sister, who is also asleep—that deep sleep of early childhood, breathing light and regular, round pink cheeks, teddy bear gripped tightly in her hands.

As she undresses, she realizes he is still not back. It's forty-five minutes since he left to drive the babysitter home. And yet she doesn't live far away. She shrugs, then slides into bed with a sigh of relief. He must be looking for a parking spot. She falls asleep as fast as her son. The next feeding is in five hours' time.

As he enters the silent apartment, his heart is speeding. He listens carefully. Not a sound. He slips into the bathroom and takes a shower. He examines his penis. It looks a little red, the skin sore. Nervously he soaps it. Then he gets out of the shower and dries himself. He rolls on deodorant and sprays himself with cologne. He does not look in the mirror. He puts on a T-shirt and a pair of boxer shorts, then goes to look at his children sleeping, as he does every night. Tonight, there is an ashy taste at the back of his throat. He forces himself not to think anymore about that furtive blow job in the woods, about that stranger's mouth sucking him, about the vague excitement he felt. He gets in bed next to his wife, who is sleeping the innocent sleep of the exhausted young mother.

⁂

A few months later, in February, she asks him sleepily as he sneaks into bed, "Why does it always take you so long to drive the babysitter home?"

In the darkness, he turns red.

"Traffic . . ."

"At this time of night?"

"There's always traffic at this time of night."

"We should try to find someone who lives locally."

"Yeah," he says.

⁂

In May, his son is six months old. He's sleeping through the night. His wife is less tired. They start making love again. But he still feels drawn by the secret world of the woods, by those women who wait there, always available. He doesn't feel as if he's cheating on his wife because those women who dispense oral pleasure in the privacy of his car have no names, no addresses, no telephone numbers. And he limits himself to fellatio with protection; he would never have intercourse with them. That would be going too far. That would be cheating on his wife. He thinks he is not cheating on her like this, because he is not penetrating another woman.

Sometimes he goes there during the day. He goes to a different forest, farther away, because he's afraid of seeing someone he knows. Instead of eating lunch with his colleagues, he drives off in his car. He now approaches these women unhesitatingly. He chooses one quickly, she gets in, he hands her the cash, and it's all over in a few minutes. He goes back to the office, filled with a growing self-disgust. He loves his wife deeply, sincerely, but he also loves these sordid desires that rise up within him, those anonymous lips, those women who never say no. He loves roaming these hot places, seeing this display of flesh, the garish makeup, the obscene lingerie. Every day, he fights against these buried urges. Every morning, when he wakes up, he tells himself he has to stop before it's too late. But each time he ends up driving to the woods, fascinated by this perverted drive-thru. He knows he could never talk to his wife about it. She wouldn't understand. She would never accept it. He can imagine all too well how her face—her very existence—would collapse if she ever found out.

Does she ever suspect, when she cooingly secures her children into their seats in the back of the car, that dozens of prostitutes have sat in her seat and have put her husband's erect penis into their mouths to make him come?

Yes, she suspects something. She thinks that the babysitter

is perhaps her husband's mistress. In June, she casually asks the girl how long it takes to drive to her house. "Ten minutes." She asks if there's much traffic on the roads, around midnight. "Hardly ever," the girl replies.

She thinks about this. So, he should be home within half an hour at most, whereas he usually takes more than an hour. She is not a naturally suspicious woman, but she is not stupid either. She is a calm person, quite mature for someone of twenty-eight. She has been married for five years and she loves her husband deeply. She has never doubted him before.

"Are you happy?" she asks him that evening.

"The happiest man in the world."

"And do you love me?"

"More than ever."

"Have you ever cheated on me?"

"Never."

"Have you ever wanted to cheat on me?"

"Never."

She looks at him steadily. He doesn't blink. He doesn't appear guilty. But she puts her plan in action, all the same, just to be sure. She borrows her sister's car for two days. She leaves her daughter with a friend for the night. She goes out to the movies and a restaurant with her husband. The babysitter looks after their son. They get home around midnight. She pays the girl. Her husband has stayed in the car, to take her home. She hears the car door bang and the engine roar. She races to her son's bedroom, picks him up, as gently as possible, and places him in a bassinet. Then she leaves the apartment, puts the baby in the backseat of

her sister's car, and gets behind the wheel. She can no longer see her husband's car, but she knows which way he is
going because she knows where the babysitter lives. After a
few minutes, she catches up with his car, and follows it
from a distance. Checking her watch, she notes that the
trip took no more than ten minutes. The metallic blue car
stops; the girl gets out, waves good-bye, types in her entry
code, and disappears through a gateway. So it's not her; the
babysitter is not the mistress. "What now?" she hisses.

To go home, he has to take the first left. But instead he
drives straight on, and he drives fast. She follows him through
dark, deserted streets. The baby is asleep. She is frightened, uneasy; her heart is pounding. But she wants—needs—
to know the truth. The woods stretch toward them, black
and tentacular. Still she tails her husband. There are lots of
cars here; she is afraid of losing him. Where is he going?
She doesn't understand. Does he have a mistress on the
other side of the woods?

Then she sees the prostitutes. Fluttering eyelids, blowing
kisses, no more than a few yards between each of them,
they flash their breasts, butts, and thighs to the passing
cars. She feels her throat tighten. In the back of the car, the
baby moans in his sleep. Her husband's car comes to a halt.
She brakes, and hears the honk of a horn from the car
behind. Quickly she overtakes him, watching her rearview
mirror, then stops a little farther on, eyes riveted to the little
reflective rectangle. She sees a prostitute get in her husband's car. The baby grumbles. He's lost his pacifier. She
doesn't hear. The blue car makes a U-turn, and hurriedly

she does the same thing, tires squealing. It turns in to an empty path. She extinguishes her headlights and drives slowly behind it. Silence descends upon the woods. She can no longer hear the raucous laughter, the traffic noise. He has switched off his engine, so she does the same. She can't see much. The baby has fallen asleep again. She gets out of her car and quietly closes the door. There is a thick carpet of moss and twigs beneath her sandals. The night air is pleasantly cool. It feels like the countryside. She walks toward the blue car.

And then the moon, as if taunting her, emerges from behind a cloud, and she sees her husband's face, contorted by pleasure. She moves closer still, her heart rent in two. Between her husband's thighs she sees a head of brown hair, busily moving up and down.

Suddenly the baby screams, loud in the night. The man jumps, opens his eyes, and sees his wife standing in front of the car. He freezes, paralyzed with horror. The prostitute lifts her head and she, too, stares speechlessly at this sad, beautiful young woman bathed in moonlight.

His wife looks at him with sorrow, with pain, with disgust. Before leaving, she removes her wedding ring and places it delicately on the hood of the car, without a word.

The Password

If we are to make reality endurable,
we must all nourish a fantasy or two.
—Marcel Proust (1871–1922),
Within a Budding Grove

Hunter Logan is rather beautiful. She has turquoise eyes—a particular color found only across the Atlantic, in certain areas of Massachussetts; an intense blue, verging on green, with flecks of gold. She also has long, fair hair that turns platinum blond in the summer. She is a slender, square-jawed American girl with a predatory smile and athletic thighs. Sometimes people tell her she looks like the actress Cameron Diaz.

Hunter came to live in Paris for a year in order to improve her French. She is taking classes at the university and staying with a cantankerous aristocratic woman on Avenue Marceau, at the corner of Rue de Bassano. It is a large, dilapidated apartment with damp bathrooms and dingy bedrooms, but as soon as she saw it Hunter fell in love with its moldings and its marble fireplace, so decorative and so very Parisian.

Madame de M. has to rent out her rooms to students in order to make ends meet. Since the death of her husband and the departure of her six children, she has not been able to bear the thought of selling this two-hundred-square-meter apartment and leaving Avenue Marceau, where she has lived for fifty years. In order to extract the maximum amount of money for the minimum amount of comfort, she rents the rooms to American students, preferably wealthy ones, who are all charmed—as Hunter was—by the view of the Arc de Triomphe, the proximity of the Champs-Élysées and the Eiffel Tower. And high-spirited eighteen-year-old Hunter is able to simply close her eyes to the tepid bathwater, the roaches, and the viscountess's sour moods.

The ban on using the landline doesn't bother her tenants either. The ingenious Savannah, from Colorado—a computer studies major who spends more time in nightclubs than in front of her laptop—managed to hack into the upstairs neighbors' Wi-Fi connection, and Hunter is able to use this, too.

⁓✤⁓

Hunter is a well-behaved young girl. Unlike Savannah, she rarely goes out. She has a boyfriend, Evan, who stayed in Boston to continue his degree in medicine, with whom she talks on Skype several times a week. The photograph of

Evan is on her bedside table. He is a serious-looking blond boy with perfect teeth. Hunter thinks she will marry him. Hunter's family is displayed above the fireplace: her parents, Jeff and Brooke; her younger sister, Holly; her brother, Thorn; and Inky the Labrador.

Sometimes, at night, staring up at the ceiling before falling asleep, she listens to the ceaseless rumble of traffic on Avenue Marceau, and the large family house on Carlton Street, which she had never left before, seems so far away that her heart aches. When she feels homesick like this, she sometimes walks down the endless hallway, the wooden floorboards creaking beneath her feet, to the huge, dusty salon with its furniture covered in white sheets. Hunter opens the rusty shutters on one of the five windows and walks out onto the balcony that runs around the entire building. Standing there and watching the city—the Place de l'Etoile, the coming and going of cars—makes her feel better.

One night, intoxicated by the indefinable odor of Paris, she felt a bony hand touch her shoulder, and gasped.

"What are you doing here?" wheezed Madame de M., dressed in an old bathrobe.

Hunter smiled. "Admiring your city," she replied in her American-accented French.

The old lady observed her for a few moments. Then a smile softened her face. "Quite right," she whispered. "You should make the most of it." Hunter was surprised to notice that Madame de M. had suddenly started using the familiar *tu* form with her.

And Madame de M. went away, leaving the young woman alone with her thoughts.

❧❧❧

Since moving to Paris, Hunter had still not gotten used to the interest she seemed to inspire in Parisian men. Even though Savannah had explained to her that all Frenchmen were obsessed by women—that this was a widely known fact she simply had to accept—she couldn't help feeling ill at ease when confronted with those insistently staring eyes, those unambiguous whispers, and sometimes, walking in the Jardin du Luxembourg, she would break into a sprint in order to escape the attentions of a lone man. Even in winter, with her wrapped up in a padded anorak, men would still find some way to hit on her. To begin with, it had been flattering. Now it was simply annoying.

As soon as the sun rose each morning, the males of Paris seemed to lose their minds. Sitting on café terraces, they spent their days watching women. Especially on the Left Bank, Hunter noticed. All it took was a bare knee on Boulevard Saint-Germain and they were thrown into a frenzy. On sunny days, Savannah and a gang of American girls more brazen than Hunter would sit outside Les Deux Magots like princesses. Older men, with suntanned faces and graying temples, would drive past in convertibles and offer them weekends in Deauville or Saint-Tropez, screen tests for a movie, the cover of a magazine. As for Hunter, she would walk back to Avenue Marceau reading *Swann in*

Love for the French literature course given by her young professor, Jerome D., at the university.

There was no denying that her professor was an attractive man. He was in his early thirties, with hazel eyes and dark brown hair. Very tall, he stood slightly stoop shouldered. He wore white shirts with the collars unbuttoned and round glasses that he would remove occasionally so he could rub the bridge of his nose. He also wore a wedding ring.

Often, Hunter noticed, there was a dark-haired young woman waiting for him in a car after his classes. Sometimes, Hunter would see two little girls in the backseat. The professor would fold up his six-foot three-inch frame, sit next to his wife and kiss her, then lean back to kiss his daughters. Hunter was always touched by this spectacle, as it reminded her of her own father and the affectionate kisses he would bestow on the whole family when he came home to Carlton Street in the evenings.

"Handsome guy," murmured another female student, standing beside Hunter and watching his car move away into traffic.

Hunter's best friend in Paris was taking the same classes as her. She was from Connecticut and her name was Taylor. She was a tall and slightly overweight brunette with surprising green eyes.

Taylor thought she was in love with the professor. Sometimes, sitting in the attic room she rented on Rue de l'Université, she would spend the whole night talking about Jerome D.'s hands, or his eyelashes, or the color of his irises.

"He's married," Hunter would repeatedly remind her.

"I know," Taylor would reply. "And his wife is beautiful."

"The brunette in the car."

"Yeah, the brunette in the car with the two little girls. A perfect family."

"You should leave families in peace."

"God, Hunter—you're so American, it makes me sad sometimes. We're in Paris. Husbands have flings here. Back home, they're all too scared. I wouldn't mind being one of the professor's flings, I can tell you that!"

"What about his wife? And his children?"

"I could care less about his wife and his children."

"And afterward?"

"Afterward? Nothing. I go home and marry a nice, fat Yank who'll give me four kids. But at least I'll have the memory of my French lover."

"I think that's disgusting."

"No man as handsome as he is can be hogged by one woman. Madame D. should have thought about that when she married him."

⁂

From her hiding place, Hunter examines Madame D.'s face. Hair tied back in a bow, high forehead, harmonious features. Taylor was right: Madame D. is beautiful. Beautiful in the way only women in their early thirties can be, with that mixture of budding maturity and still tangible youthfulness. She is elegant, too, in her black suit and stiletto heels. A true Parisian lady.

Concealed behind a tree, Hunter is close enough to the professor's wife to see that she appears worried, her forehead wrinkled by faint lines. She sighs. Leaning against her car, she chews on her key fob. The little girls aren't with her today.

Students swarm from the building and divide into small groups on the sidewalk. The professor is a head taller than the crowd around him. His wife spots him, opens the door, and sits behind the steering wheel. He joins her. She doesn't look at him. Hunter notices that they do not kiss. The car speeds away.

Hunter waits for Taylor.

"Did you skip class?" Taylor asks when she arrives.

"No, I got here too late. I was waiting for you."

Taylor is exultant. "Hey, guess what? The professor's a womanizer!"

"How do you know?"

"I met a girl who slept with him. Apparently he's famous for it. All you have to do is go to his office, do a bit of flirting, and wham bam thank you ma'am!"

Hunter remains silent. She thinks about the little girls in the back of the car, and of Madame D.'s somber face. She doesn't know why, but she wants to cry.

❧

"Miss Logan?"

She turns around and she is caught in the full glare of the professor's charming smile.

"Do you live near here?" he asks, gesturing to Place Saint-Sulpice.

She stands up. "No, I live on Avenue Marceau."

He sits down, and she follows suit.

"So, you must be staying with the viscountess."

"Yes," Hunter admits, feeling intimidated.

The fountain beside them makes a pretty, musical sound.

"I often go for walks in the Luxembourg," she says. "With Proust."

"Good idea."

She can feel his golden-brown gaze touching her cheeks, her forehead, her lips.

"By the way, your last essay was excellent, if I remember correctly."

"Thank you."

"You don't have to thank me. It was very well written."

She looks up at him, blushing slightly.

He says, "We could go for a drink if you like."

She can no longer hear the fountain, only the sound of his voice.

"There's a nice café just over there. What do you say?"

She notices he is carrying a large folder.

"You know what this is?" he asks.

"No."

"Guess."

"Your next class?"

"Wrong! It's a book."

"On Proust?"

He laughs. "No, I've already done that! This is a novel. My first novel."

"Do you have a publisher?"

"Yes. These are the final proofs. I'm correcting them at the moment. I was on my way to see my publisher when I met you."

"Will it be published soon?"

"In the fall."

"What's it about?"

"Love."

Hunter feels herself blush again.

The professor smiles as he looks at her. Then he strokes her cheek. "How pretty you are, Miss Logan. And how afraid of me you seem!"

"No," she says, standing up again. "I'm not afraid of you."

"And yet you're trembling. . . ."

He takes her hand in his. He's right: she is trembling.

"I'm not going to eat you."

"Please . . ."

The professor lets go of her hand. "Relax."

She says nothing.

"Let's go for a walk in the Luxembourg. Just the three of us: you, me, and Marcel."

⁂

Hunter wished the huge yellowish clawfoot bathtub in which she lay would swallow her. The water was no longer even tepid; it was just plain cold.

Savannah hammered at the bathroom door. "Hey, Boston, have you drowned in there? Your pal Taylor has called three times tonight!"

"I'm coming," Hunter muttered.

She emerged from the tub and wrapped herself in a towel. Then she lay on the floor, her feet raised up on the bidet. She dreaded talking to Taylor, who would undoubtedly guess that she was hiding something.

It all began yesterday, in the Luxembourg. The two of them walked under the chestnut trees. The weather was perfect. Around them, people were playing tennis, running, sunbathing. Jerome D. told her about his book. She listened dreamily. He held her hand, and she made no objection. She had the impression that people were looking at them kindly, as if they were happily in love, and this thrilled her.

Then he kissed her. Intoxicated, she let him. For a brief instant the sad face of Madame D. and her little girls flashed through Hunter's mind. Then Evan's face, too. But she pushed them away. It was only a kiss, after all. . . .

But the kiss did not end. It became less innocent. In the shadow of a chestnut tree, Jerome D. became bolder. His hands brushed her breasts, her hips. He rubbed himself against her, drank in her kiss.

"I have an apartment, on Rue de Vaugirard," he whispered into her hair. "You want to come? It's nice there."

Hunter stiffened.

"What's the matter?" Jerome D. asked.

Hunter freed herself from his embrace. "You're married."

He laughed. "So?"

She looked at him, dumbfounded. "But . . . b-b-but . . . ," she stammered.

He drew her close to him again. "My wife doesn't know anything."

Hunter pushed him away. "How do you know?"

Surprised, he looked at her more attentively. "I'm sure she doesn't."

Hunter took a few steps back. "I think your wife looks sad. She knows you're cheating on her."

He laughed again. "So you think this is cheating, do you? A little kiss on a sunny afternoon? Seemed to me you were rather enjoying it—"

"Everyone in the university says you have affairs with your students."

He smiled mockingly. "Oh, so you're worried about my bad reputation?"

"I'm not afraid of you or your reputation. I despise you. If you were my husband, or my father, I would be ashamed."

Jerome D. gave her a sardonic look. "Poor little American girl," he hissed. "You really need to get laid more often!"

Then, with a shrug, and a quick adjustment of his shirt collar, he walked away.

❧

Jerome D.'s book was published. It was displayed in bookstore windows and the author's photograph appeared in the newspapers. The university organized a book-signing event, which was a great success. Hunter was the only student in the class who didn't want to buy the professor's novel.

Ever since the incident in the Luxembourg, she had felt disgusted by Jerome D., and her aversion was accentuated by the fact that he slept with Taylor not long afterward. Taylor quickly guessed that something must have happened between Hunter and the professor. When he gave a lower grade for one of Hunter's essays, Taylor realized the truth.

"You shouldn't have turned him down."

"Oh, so you have to say yes and be screwed in his whore-house on Rue de Vaugirard to be given good grades?"

Shocked by such vulgarities coming from Hunter's usually prim mouth, Taylor blushed and said nothing.

❧

Hunter stood in a corridor, on the lookout for Professor D. As soon as he emerged from a classroom, she cornered him.

"Excuse me, monsieur, but what is this grade supposed to mean?" she demanded, holding up her essay.

Irritated and in a rush, Jerome D. almost barked at her: "it means, Miss Logan, that your work wasn't good."

Unflustered, Hunter stood in his way. "So you wouldn't mind if I showed my essay to some other professors? I'd like to know if they find it as poor as you did."

Jerome D. hesitated.

Hunter attacked: "I can't go back to America with a grade like that in my file. It's unacceptable. You know perfectly well that it was a good essay. You also know why you gave me that grade. I want you to change it. If you don't, I'll file a complaint against you."

Jerome D. bared his white teeth. "Are you saying you would accuse me of what you Americans call 'sexual harassment'? Are you planning on spreading this fib among my colleagues?"

"Certainly."

"Believe me, in France that kind of puritan bullshit is considered laughable. No one here takes feminists seriously. As you will learn to your cost."

"Je pense . . . vous allez . . ." Abandoning her usual reserve, Hunter ran out of French words and switched to her more reliable, more fluid mother tongue. *"You're going to regret this for the rest of your life."*

"Oh really? How terrifying," Jerome D. snickered.

Her face hot and red, she turned on her heels and walked away, the professor's laughter echoing in her ears. Outside, Madame D. was waiting in her car. Hunter walked past her without a glance, fists balled.

An article in a popular women's magazine was what finally sent her over the edge.

Love Scenes, a debut novel by a young literature professor, has made a big impact in the literary world. Jerome D., who teaches at a large Parisian university, has written an apologia for marriage and fidelity. With humor and emotion, his book traces the history of a marriage, from its beginnings, through its pitfalls and joys, to its ruin and finally its rebirth. Married with two children—Albertine, 4, and Odette, 2—this handsome 34-year-old insists he wrote the book for his wife and daughters. "In the age we live in, people have stopped believing in marriage. There are more and more divorces and separations, and it's the children who suffer. I wanted to write something romantic, even if that might seem old-fashioned now. I invented a story with a happy ending, something that will give people back some hope and joy in this time of crisis and gloom." Such is Jerome D.'s novel, written with a subtlety and nostalgia inspired by his hero Marcel Proust, blended with a verve that is all his own.

Beneath a large photograph of Jerome D. at his desk, one of his daughters sitting on his lap, was the following caption: "Jerome D. pictured with his elder daughter, Albertine."

Hunter almost choked. This was too much! As she paced her bedroom, her eyes fell on the photo of Evan. For a few seconds she stared at the young man's face. How would she react, she wondered, if Evan ever cheated on her after they were married? Then she studied the photograph of her father, examined his craggy face, his kindly eyes, his reassuring smile. Hunter felt sure he would never do such a thing to his wife.

Now she looked more closely at the portrait of Jerome D.

in the newspaper. She despised that face, those eyes, that smile. She felt sorry for the daughter. The professor deserved to be taught a lesson.

Visible behind Jerome D.'s right shoulder in the picture was his computer screen. Hunter grabbed a magnifying glass, which Madame de M. used for her stamp collection, and held it in front of the photograph. On the screen, Hunter recognized the logo of a Facebook page.

She thought for a few moments. Then she ran out of the room and down the hallway to bang on Savannah's door.

A corpselike voice replied, "Who the hell is that? It's ten am!"

"Open up! It's Hunter."

"You have to be kidding. I only went to bed three hours ago."

"Please! I need to pick your brain."

"My brain is still pickled at this time in the morning. Leave me alone!"

"Open the door and I'll lend you my new dress."

Silence. Hunter listened intently.

Then Savannah's crumpled face, framed by an unruly mop of hair, appeared in the doorway.

"Seriously? I thought you didn't want to lend it to me."

"Well, now I do. But only if you help me."

"Okay," said Savannah.

"I want to get onto a guy's Facebook page," Hunter told her.

"What's his name?"

Savannah typed the letters into her computer. "All right,

so this is his profile . . . Jerome D. . . . Wow, not bad! Do you have his e-mail address?"

"Yes, he gave it to us at the start of the year. He's my professor."

"Hmm . . . is this sexual, by any chance? Anyway, I need the password."

"Can I try more than once?"

"You have six attempts. After that, it blocks you. And it's not easy, finding a password. It's not like a code—you can't use pure reason to find it. Passwords usually have more to do with the heart than the head. It's a whole different ball game. I'm no good at passwords—I'm too cerebral, you know? So, in case this doesn't work out . . . you'll lend me your dress anyway, right?"

"Try this."

She handed a sheet of paper to Savannah, who read out loud: "'Swann, Guermantes, Marcel, Combray, madeleine—'" She interjected: "Bit intellectual, don't you think?"

"He *is* an intellectual."

Savannah tried each word, finishing with, "Nope, not that either."

"Try *catleya*."

"What?"

"*C-a-t-l-e-y-a.*"

"What the hell's that?"

"A flower."

"A flower?"

"Read *Swann in Love* and you'll understand."

"Who *in Love*?"

"It's Proust. I told you, my professor is a Proustian. Try *catleya*—it means 'making out.' Go on, type it."

"This is our last chance. After this, it'll block us."

Savannah obeyed. After a few minutes, her eyes widened with disbelief.

"Whoa!"

"What?"

"We're in! You cracked the code."

"I knew it."

"I'm impressed, Hunter Logan. I would never have thought you had it in you. So . . . let's see what this guy has in his private messages."

The keys of her computer made small clicking noises under her fingertips.

"What a dick—he hasn't deleted anything! Oh, look at this. . . . The rogue!"

Mesmerized, Hunter leaned close to the screen.

"He has a date this evening with a certain Oriane. Hotel D., room 208. She's supposed to wait for him in a garter belt. . . . Ooh, sexy! And look at this—'Miss Rosemonde,' who he met yesterday at Rue de Vaugirard. . . . My God, have you seen how many meetings he's made in his apartment? Your professor is quite the Casanova. And you say he's married? Can't say I'm surprised. The married ones are always the worst, in this city. Believe me, I know what I'm talking about."

Hunter's eyes scanned the words on the screen: words of love and lust, names and addresses, a seemingly endless list. . . .

Savannah giggled.

"Can you print this for me?" Hunter asked.

"Sure!"

While the printer hummed away, Hunter looked for his mailing address on the online directory. She found it and wrote it down. Savannah handed her a sheaf of about twenty pages.

"What are you going to do with all this? It's dynamite."

"If I lend you my necklace, will you promise to keep your mouth shut about this? To forget it ever happened?"

Savannah looked at her. "Nothing bad, though . . . right, Hunter?"

"Don't worry. I know what I'm doing. And it's for a good cause."

Hunter smiled and slid the pages into an envelope.

❧

Standing in front of a mailbox on Avenue Denfert-Rochereau, Hunter did not even hesitate for a second before pushing the thick envelope through the slot.

On the envelope, she had written:

Madame Jerome D.
3 Rue Cassini
Paris 75014

The USB Key

Nearly all men resemble those vast, empty mansions
where the owner occupies only a few rooms
and never sets foot in the sealed-off wings.
—François Mauriac (1885–1970), *Diary*

When I came home, the USB key was on the living-room coffee table. Next to it was a white Post-it note: "For Thérèse."

The handwriting was that of my husband, Hubert. I took Luc out of his romper, then put him in the playpen in his bedroom.

I switched on the computer and plugged in the USB key.

To begin with, there was nothing. Then the video started. Our couch. The same one I was sitting on now. The empty couch. Silence. Then, a figure walked into view. It was Hubert. He seemed to be thinking of what to say. Finally, I heard his voice, slightly distorted by the recording.

"Thérèse, I know what I have to say will hurt you. But I have no choice. I must tell you the truth. I'm not good with words—I don't feel capable of writing you a letter. I don't know how to tell you what I've done. I daren't tell you to your face. So I came up with this solution: recording myself as if I were talking to you. Yes, I know, it's a coward's way out. But I *am* a coward, Thérèse—you just didn't know it."

I paused the video. Hubert froze on the screen. I looked at his blond hair, his clear-eyed gaze, his tortoiseshell glasses: the open, normal, good-looking face of a young father.

The baby was gurgling in his bedroom, playing with a musical box. I continued to examine Hubert's face. What else was he going to tell me? I thought I knew everything. He'd already confessed.

I had found a credit card receipt in his jacket one month before this. It was for a hotel in Biarritz, and the date was on a weekend when he'd told me he was in Bordeaux on a work trip.

I had handed him the receipt and his face had fallen. He had taken me in his arms, crying and mumbling some story about a girl who meant nothing to him. A momentary lapse. The first infidelity in a marriage that was only three years old. He swore to me he would never do it again. It was difficult, but I forgave him. I thought of our son. I didn't want to sacrifice our marriage for a mere fling. Other women had always warned me that all wives must expect to be cheated on one day or another. That was life. That was marriage. My parents' marriage had been the same, and his parents', too. Close your eyes to the husband's misdemeanors.

"That's just how men are, my dear," my mother had told me. "Incapable of being faithful. They're like rutting beasts. Women don't have the same instincts. We're more moderate, monogamous. When a man cheats on his wife, it's no big deal. But when a woman cheats on her husband, the opposite is true. She is considered a fallen woman. For a man, though . . . it's just in his nature. You have to understand that, accept it."

And that's what I did. I forgave Hubert for the one-night stand he'd had in that Biarritz hotel, while I had imagined him working in Bordeaux. I wanted to turn the page. I didn't want to talk about it. I never even asked him for her name.

I think he was relieved by my reaction. He must have feared a big scene—sobbing, screaming, the usual things that women do when they find out about a husband's infidelity. Maybe he thought I would pack my bags and leave with the baby. But no, I remained the same—I hid my wounds, suffered in silence. I prayed that it would never happen again. I was afraid my calmness would desert me, the second time around.

I pressed "Play." Hubert's petrified face came back to life.

"You thought I had a mistress. I can still see you handing me that credit card receipt. You said, 'What were you doing at a hotel in Biarritz?' You were pale and trembling. I was ashamed. So I lied. Made up a story about another woman. You never even opened your mouth. Our son was crying in his crib. You went to console him. He had a fever. Once he fell asleep, you came back to the living room. You sat on the couch. You asked me questions. I answered them. With lies. What did I tell you? That I didn't love her, that it was a one-night stand. Then you asked me why I'd married you. I told you—and I repeat this now—I married you because I loved you. But I had a secret. Something that's been buried inside me for years. I love men, Thérèse. I've always hidden it—from you, and from everyone else I know. I've fought against it as best I could. I tortured myself, forced myself not to give in. I had a few brief affairs with women during our marriage—mainly because I was trying to prove to myself that I wasn't homosexual. But I am. And, at thirty years old, I have to accept the fact. Even if it destroys my marriage—and you with it."

I got up so I wouldn't have to keep looking at his face. While he spoke, I looked out of the window. It was raining. Gusts of wind shook the trees. Night fell. Hubert's voice, broken by emotion, continued to reel off his sordid confession.

"I'm leaving you because I'm in love with a man. There—I've said it. You'll hate me for saying it, despise me. You don't know this man. You are strong, Thérèse. You are a woman. I believe women are stronger than men. I want to believe that to make myself feel less guilty. To spare myself the shame of having ruined your life. The next day, you said to me, 'I forgive you. You were weak. It's human. But I love you and I want us to raise our son together.' I realized then I would have to tell you the truth. Even if you hadn't found that receipt, I would still have told you. I shudder to think of how other people will react: your parents, my parents, our friends. I think about everything you'll have to go through. I think about our son. He's so young. I tell myself I should just leave, without writing a letter or making any kind of explanation, that you would find out in the end anyway. But I owe you the truth."

I moved away from the window and sat down again, but with my back to the screen. I found it impossible to look at his face.

"I think I've always preferred men, without ever accepting it. When I was fourteen, I used to masturbate with a friend from my class. I wasn't interested in girls. He used to buy magazines full of naked women and he would get hard, looking at them. But not me. What got me hard was looking at him. I slept with a man for the first time when I was eighteen. And I liked it. I prefer men's bodies—those masculine smells, those hard edges. I tried to talk to my parents about it. I felt dirty, guilty, perverted. But they didn't want to hear what I had to say. Or rather, they were afraid to. They just shut me out, and left me to my demons. Then I met you, after several years of wandering and doubts. You were beautiful and sweet. You still are. I thought: a woman like that could save me, could get me out of this nightmare. With her, I could be a normal man. A married man. A father. So, for three years, I tried to play that role. I did my best, Thérèse. Strangely, I never had to force myself to make love with you. With you, it felt natural and beautiful. It was innocent, tender. But it wasn't sexual. For me, it wasn't really making love. Simply because you're a woman and I prefer men. There were nights when I woke up in a cold sweat: you were sleeping next to me, so peaceful, so happy, and I wanted so much to confide in you, to tell you what was tormenting me. Then you became pregnant, and the idea of spilling all the vileness that tortured me to a woman whose belly was so perfect and round seemed monstrous. I felt a thrill run through me whenever I saw a man I liked. I would surf the Internet, watching videos of men having sex. I would do that when you were away. It really excited me. I told myself I was sick, abnormal. I would be seized by terrible desires. I had to stifle them, suppress them. Finally, I couldn't stand it any longer. I began hanging around in places where homosexuals go. There were public toilets with holes in the cubicle walls. The holes were quite low down. I didn't understand what they were for. Then I saw a man put his penis through one of those holes. On the other side of the wall, a stranger's mouth sucked it. I was horrified and turned on. I ran out of there, my head full of furtive images. I also went to a gay nightclub. The men there were kissing each other on the mouth, caressing each other openly, slow dancing together. That was where I met Phili."

I turned to face the screen. Hubert was speaking in a new voice, less hesitant. His gaze had softened.

"I think he looks like Daniel Day-Lewis in *My Beautiful Laundrette*. He's tall and slim, and he loves life. He taught me not to be ashamed of my difference, not to be ashamed of my desires. It's true—before I met him, I felt ashamed all the time. I felt marginal, excluded, alone. Now, I'm at peace with myself. I understand what I want. The weekend in

Biarritz, I was with Phili. We went to Arcachon, too, on a different weekend."

For the first time since beginning his confession, Hubert paused. He changed position, lit a cigarette. He took a few drags, then stubbed it out.

The baby was still babbling in his playpen. Soon he would want dinner, and I hadn't bathed him yet. How much longer would this video last?

As if in reply to my unasked question, Hubert went on:

"Don't worry, I've almost finished. I know you have to look after Luc. It's not a good time for you. Forgive me. I wanted to tell you this, too. I think that, when a man loves other men, they often change partners. There's a sexual hunger. After him, there will be others. And then one day, I hope, there will be the man of my life. The man who will love me. The man I'll love. It's okay—I'm taking precautions. I'm not crazy. I don't have AIDS. I've taken the test several times. Look. . . ."

He took a sheet of paper from his pocket and held it up to the camera. I was able to make out his name, the date, and the words "HIV negative."

"I can imagine you on the other side of the screen. I can imagine you, feeling heartbroken. Sickened. Revolted. I'm sure it never even crossed your mind that I might be homosexual. It must be a terrible shock for you. If it was another woman, okay—that's easier to accept. But a homosexual husband? No. It could scar you for life. You know everything about me now, Thérèse. Have you managed to listen to this confession to the end? Will you be able to understand? I don't know. I suppose we'll get a divorce, that our marriage is over. Will you agree to see me again? Will you let me see my son, help you bring him up? And will you let me see you, too, from time to time? I really hope you will. Tell me what you want. Your wish is my command, Thérèse. I'll call you at eight o'clock tonight, after Luc has gone to bed. If you don't answer, I'll understand that you don't want to see me anymore. And I will try to accept your decision."

Hubert's voice broke. He hid his face in his hands and wept for a long time, in silence. For a short while, he remained sitting on the couch. Then he stood up and moved toward the camera. Before the screen went black, I heard his voice one last time:

"Please, Thérèse, destroy this USB key. Thank you."

The woman who looked back at me from the mirror was a stranger. She had a vague resemblance to me, her hair in particular. But her face was completely unknown to me. There were deep lines stretching from her nose to her mouth; her eyes were dull and lifeless; her complexion was waxy, almost greenish. I didn't know her, but at the same time, there was something familiar about her.

When this woman started at the sound of a baby's cry, I understood who she was. The woman gently bathed him, then gave him his dinner. She was tender with the child. She put him to bed. Then she sat next to the telephone and waited.

At exactly eight o'clock, it rang. She picked up the receiver.

A man's voice said, "It's me."

She replied, "I know it's you."

Even her voice was not like mine.

"Thérèse, I—"

"No, I don't want to talk about it on the phone. I want you to come here. Now. We can talk then. I'll wait for you."

The man said, "I'm on my way."

The unknown woman stood up, then looked at me in the mirror.

I asked her, "What are you going to say to him?"

She rearranged her hair, adjusted her blouse.

"That I don't want a divorce."

"What? But your husband is a homosexual!"

"Maybe, but he's still my husband. He's the father of my child. I bear his name, and so does our son. I won't agree to divorce him. I won't let him leave Luc and me. Just because he's homosexual doesn't mean he can't be a good father. I want a real home for my son. Away from home, he can have his secret life, his lovers, his movies, his nights out. But here, he will be a father and a husband. That's all I ask of him."

"What if he refuses?"

"He said he would do whatever I want."

She looked at me. I had never seen such a hard look before.

Then she declared, "He'll want this, or he'll never see his son again."

There was a knock at the door.

We looked at each other for a long time. She was quite beautiful, with her ravaged, noble face.

"Answer the door," she told me. "Hold your head up proudly, Thérèse. And whatever you do, keep your eyes dry."

THE BRUNETTE FROM RUE RAYNOUARD

Those who truly love doubt nothing,
or doubt all
                    —HONORÉ DE BALZAC (1799–1850),
                              A Murky Business

E ugénie? Hey, is this a bad time?"

"Hi, Eve! No, it's fine—I'm just finishing up a case."

"Listen, I'm not sure how to tell you this, but . . . well, we've known each other a long time. . . ."

"What is it?"

"I wasn't sure I should tell you, but then I thought you would have done the same for me. . . ."

"Okay. Go on. What is this about?"

"Are you alone?"

"Yeah. I'm in my office."

"Okay. It's about Lionel. This may seem strange, but I can't keep quiet about it any longer."

"Just tell me, for God's sake!"

"All right. Several times now, I've seen your husband enter a building near my office during the lunch hour. To start with, I wasn't worried—I just assumed that Lionel must have a business meeting in the area. But the longer it's gone on, the shadier it's seemed."

"Where is this building?"

"Rue Raynouard."

"And why do you think it's shady?"

"Because when he comes out, he's red-faced. And he walks away quickly, with his head down. He doesn't seem normal."

"..."

"Hello, Eugénie? Are you still there?"

"Yes. So why didn't you tell me earlier?"

"I thought about it. I knew that, since last year—since your thing with . . . —anyway, since all that, I know you've had a tough time. I didn't want to make things worse. But it must have happened about ten times now, so I thought it would be better to let you know."

"Ten times! I don't know what to think."

"Do you think he . . . ?"

"It's possible. After all he went through with the other thing, after what I did . . ."

"How does he seem at the moment?"

"Quiet. Preoccupied. But no more than usual, you know. He's never been very talkative, my husband."

"There's something else I have to tell you."

"..."

"Eugénie, are you okay? I feel like I should tell you everything."

"Oh my God . . . What are you going to tell me now? Go ahead. . . ."

"I ended up going down to the building's intercom and looking at the list of names. I thought maybe he had a medical appointment or something. Do you know if that's the case?"

"No. Definitely not. He's never mentioned it."

" . . ."

"Eve? Keep going."

"Okay, so there were no doctors on the list. Or physios. Nothing like that at all. And then . . ."

"What?"

"I saw Lionel go into a woman's apartment. In that building."

"How could you have seen that?"

"You're going to think I'm crazy, but . . . I followed him."

"Jesus. Did he see you?"

"Of course not. I was wearing a knit cap, with a hoodie over it. There's no way he could have recognized me. He pressed a button on the intercom—the initials 'F. G.' I followed him in. That woman lives on the first floor. I pretended to wait for the elevator. When she opened the door, I got a quick look at her."

"So? What's she like?"

"Well, that's why I'm calling you, Eugénie."

"Will you just spit it out? The suspense is killing me!"

"I'm just worried about hurting you."

"What, is she gorgeous?"

"Yes, Eugénie, she's gorgeous. And . . . sexy."

"Meaning what?"

"Don't get annoyed. I just mean she's sexy. Tight skirt, but chic. High heels. Nice hair. I caught a glimpse of a pink-and-white entry hall, very feminine looking, with books on shelves and watercolors on the walls."

"Shit."

"Yeah, shit."

"I'm glad you told me. Even if I have a very bad feeling about this."

"How are things between you and Lionel?"

"You mean since . . . since all that?"

"Yeah, since all that."

"Not good. Not good at all. We never talk about it. I can tell he's hurting. But he has his work, and he's busy looking after the kids and me. He never mentions it, and I don't dare bring it up. I had actually started to believe that it was all behind us, that we'd turned the corner. But now, after what you've told me, I'm wondering whether that's true."

"And what about . . . as a couple?"

"In bed, you mean?"

"Yes, in bed."

"There's not much to tell. He's tired. I'm tired. Just like any other couple who've been married for a while and who've been through what we've been through, I imagine."

"What are you going to do?"

"I don't know."

"Are you going to talk to him about it?"

"No. Not right now."

"You're not mad at me, are you?"

"No."

"You promise?"

"Yes. Just give me the number on Rue Raynouard. Thank you. Thank you, Eve."

～❦～

"Eve? It's me."

"Hang on, I'm just coming out of a meeting. Can you hold for a couple of seconds? . . . Hello? Okay, I can talk now."

"Do you have five minutes?"

"Sure, go ahead. I've been expecting your call. Are you okay, by the way? You sound a little strange."

"Yes, I'm okay. I'm just a bit . . . Well, you'll understand. Where to begin?"

"You went to that F. G.'s place, on Rue Raynouard?"

"Yes. Not long after your call. I stayed in my car, out in front of the building. I didn't see Lionel. After a while, F. G. came out. She was just as you described her. A beautiful woman. I almost stayed in the car, because I felt afraid, but in the end I got out and followed her. I watched her, that woman, with her sensual walk, and I felt sick at heart because I was thinking to myself, She's my husband's mistress. He makes love with her, but with me nothing happens anymore. I could imagine Lionel's hands touching her long brown hair, her soft skin, her hips, and I felt like crying. It's all my fault, Eve."

"Don't say that, Eugénie. There's no point torturing yourself."

"If only I hadn't had that stupid fling. If only I hadn't . . ."

"You have to forget all that—you know you do."

"I followed her to Place du Trocadéro. She sat in one of those big cafés. She looked at her cell phone and smiled. I imagined she had just received a text from Lionel. I sat at a table not too far from her. I could see her sparkling eyes, that pale, luminous skin. How could I hope to compete with a woman like that? I felt lost. I didn't dare confront her. What could I have said? So I went home."

"And then?"

"When Lionel came home, I noticed that he was spending a lot of time on his phone. I wanted to make love that night. He turned me down. He did it nicely, but . . . obviously he doesn't find me attractive anymore. I don't do anything for him now. But how could I, next to her? Anyway, that night, while he was sleeping, I looked through the messages on his phone. There were lots of texts sent to 'F. G.' I didn't have time to read them, but I saw the word 'sex' in the first one. That was enough."

"Stop. You're upsetting yourself—"

"If only I hadn't gotten involved with that guy—"

"There's no point dwelling on that. Just try to calm down. Think about what you're going to do next. Will you talk to Lionel? Tell him that you know?"

"But what can I say to him, really? He went through so much pain because of me. If he's cheating on me with this F. G., it's my fault. It's all my fault. I'm going to hang up now. I can't bear to talk about it anymore. Bye. . . ."

❀

"Is this Madame F. G.?"

"Who's that?"

" . . . "

"Who are you?"

"I'm Lionel's wife. Eugénie. I know my husband is with you. He went in there ten minutes ago. I saw him. I'd like to talk to you—to both of you. Please open the door."

'I'm sorry, but that's impossible, madame."

"I'm not going to tell you my life story on the intercom; it's ridiculous. Give Lionel and me a chance. Just a little chance. Leave him to me. Let me try to make him happy. He probably told you about my stupid affair. I will regret it for the rest of my life. I know it hurt him. He's been distant from me ever since. Oh God, what a mess I am, crying outside your door. You must think me pathetic. I would like to come in and speak to you, to him."

"Madame, please stop crying. Calm down."

"Is Lionel with you? Is he listening?"

"I'm going to hang up now. Good-bye, madame."

❀

Lionel. I know you're with that F. G. woman.

I saw you going into her apartment. She wouldn't let me in.

LIONEL PLEASE REPLY TO MY TEXTS!

Calm down, Eugénie. Let me explain.

Don't bother.

Where are you?

In a café.

Tell me where you are. I'll meet you there.

Why? To tell me that you're in love with F. G.?

To talk to you.

I already know what's going on.

I'll explain about F. G.

What's the point?

*I want to tell you how much F. G. has helped me,
restored my self-confidence.*

Stop.

*No, this is important, Eugénie.
I want you to meet her.*

What the hell is wrong with you?
Why would you want that?

Because she's saved me in these last 6 months.

6 MONTHS?
You've been sleeping with her for 6 MONTHS?

Eugénie, you've got this all wrong!
You don't understand.

I understand that you love another woman.

No. I love YOU.

??

I want you to see her with me.
She would like that, too.

WTF! You want a threesome?
Have you lost your fucking mind?

Please calm down.

This hurts SO MUCH.

Just tell me where you are please.
I'll be there in five minutes.

NO.

OK, Eugénie, enough. Please stop arguing and
just read what I'm going to write:
F. G. = Dr. Frances-Sarah Guidoboni, SEX
THERAPIST, 47 Rue Raynouard. I've seen her
one hour per week since you admitted your one-
night stand. I had difficulties after that, in bed.
Now tell me where you are. I want to hold you tight
and tell you how much I love you. I want you.